# THE HORSEMEN GATHER

# THE HORSEMEN GATHER

## THE UNBELIEVABLE MR. BROWNSTONE™ BOOK SEVENTEEN

### MICHAEL ANDERLE

The Horsemen Gather (this book) is a work of fiction. All of the characters, organizations, and events portrayed in this novel are either products of the author's imagination or are used fictitiously. Sometimes both.

Copyright © 2019 Michael Anderle
Cover by Andrew Dobell, www.creativeedgestudios.co.uk
Cover copyright © LMBPN Publishing
A Michael Anderle Production

LMBPN Publishing supports the right to free expression and the value of copyright. The purpose of copyright is to encourage writers and artists to produce the creative works that enrich our culture.

The distribution of this book without permission is a theft of the author's intellectual property. If you would like permission to use material from the book (other than for review purposes), please contact support@lmbpn.com. Thank you for your support of the author's rights.

LMBPN Publishing
PMB 196, 2540 South Maryland Pkwy
Las Vegas, NV 89109

First US edition, March 2019
Version 1.01 April 2019

The Oriceran Universe (and what happens within / characters / situations / worlds) are Copyright (c) 2017-19 by Martha Carr and LMBPN Publishing.

THE HORSEMEN GATHER TEAM

**Special Thanks**
to Mike Ross
for BBQ Consulting
Jessie Rae's BBQ - Las Vegas, NV

**Thanks to the JIT Readers**

Diane L. Smith
Keith Verret
Nicole Emens
Daniel Weigert
Peter Manis
Jeff Eaton
Kelly O'Donnell
John Ashmore
James Caplan
Angel LaVey
Larry Omans
Micky Cocker
Misty Roa
Paul Westman

*If I've missed anyone, please let me know!*

**Editor**
Lynne Stiegler

*To Family, Friends and
Those Who Love
to Read.
May We All Enjoy Grace
to Live the Life We Are
Called.*

## CHAPTER ONE

F our drones flew overhead in tight formation in the cloudless sky. One machine broke away and descended, a small white box clutched in its cargo arms as it made a sharp right turn. It passed over James and Thomas, a dull buzz announcing its arrival.

*Here it comes,* James thought. *It had to be four of them.*

Thomas barked at the low-flying Andercarr delivery drone. He strained against his leash and growled, ready to take down the mechanical menace that dared to invade his neighborhood. The dog had nothing against birds, but he despised drones with an almost rabid passion. James had had to stop him from taking down a drone making a delivery a few weeks before. It was funny until the delivery company stopped by to complain.

"It's okay, boy," James rumbled, keeping a firm grip on the leash. "It's just someone getting a package. You don't want to stop someone from getting their As Seen on TV shit. That could be the only thing they have going for them."

Thomas continued to bark at the drone.

Between magic and drones, James wondered about the future of human drivers. The main thing keeping drones from eliminating their flesh competitors was the fact that most cities didn't want hovering robots carrying anything heavy around, especially since hackers had long since proven that the much-vaunted security systems of delivery companies weren't foolproof. A few high-profile so-called accidents had ended the brief risk of drones cluttering the sky with every type of cargo imaginable, but there were still more than enough that James couldn't go for a walk without his dog getting pissed off.

*Will it make a difference if they start doing a bunch of shit with magic?*

Thomas growled and crouched low as if trying to figure out if he could make it into the air to take down the drone. James wouldn't put it past the animal to try some doggie parkour to get at his prey.

*It might be fun to see him try, but I can't piss off the delivery companies. I order too much shit, especially for PFW.*

"Come on, boy," James tugged on Thomas' leash. "Let's finish our walk. The drones will be gone by then."

Thomas finally gave up on the aerial enemy. The dog barked a few more times before turning to follow his master as they continued their walk.

At least the warm sun kept James from needing a coat. That was one of the great bonuses about living in Los Angeles. Not every city stayed as warm in late October.

People bitched about how it almost never snowed in the winter. It had only snowed here twice in his entire life, but he saw that as a bonus. Every trip to a cold climate reinforced the opinion.

"Should probably buy some fucking candy," James mumbled. "Halloween's coming up."

Thomas looked at him and barked once.

James hadn't cared about the holiday in past years, but the last time he'd talked to Alison, she suggested he could stand to be a little user-friendly with the neighborhood kids. His increased visible presence in the neighborhood, including throwing barbeques, meant that people now expected him to be more social all the time.

*Being nice to people makes shit more complicated, but it does make the neighborhood better.*

"Complicated." James grunted. "Can you believe that shit, Thomas? This is what I get for not keeping shit simple. Now I have to worry about fucking *candy*."

The dog barked and wagged his tail as they got close to the park. James liked this time of day; it was a little bit before the neighborhood kids got home from school and flooded the park with their games. His attempts to go to the park when the neighborhood kids were around always turned annoying. The children swarmed Thomas, eager to pet the dog.

They had dubbed him "the Granite Fido." The dog loved the attention, but his master didn't.

*He doesn't even do bounties. He's just a dog.*

James stared at his dog for a moment, considering a few possibilities.

*Then again, maybe I could get him some body armor. Would a defensive artifact work on a dog? Zoe could mix up some sort of potion that would help him bite harder. With a shield and a good bite, he could help me take down bounty assholes.*

James rubbed his chin as he considered ways to turn his dog into a bounty hunting aid before discarding the idea. No matter how tough he made Thomas with artifacts or armor, the dog wouldn't be able to deal with the high-level bounties who now formed the bounty hunter's main prey. He'd get hurt, and it'd be his master's fault.

A woman's scream ripped from a stand of trees, blasting the idle thoughts about turning Thomas into a killing machine out of James' head.

*What the fuck? Someone is seriously trying shit in my neighborhood?*

James frowned and released the leash as he sprinted toward the source of the scream. Thomas barked several times and charged forward, his legs pumping hard.

A loud thud came from the trees, cutting off another scream. When James arrived, a man was standing over a woman who was lying on the ground clutching her bleeding head. The man held her purse, and he wore brass knuckles.

"You should have just given it to me, bitch!" the mugger screamed. "Getting hurt was your own damned fault." He turned at the sound of Thomas' barking. "What the fuck now?"

The dog leapt at the man and sank his teeth into his thigh.

The man squealed in pain and tried to shake the dog off, but soon collapsed to the ground slapping his hands against the ground. "Get him off me. Get him off me."

*If he had more discipline, he might have thought to punch*

*Thomas. But then he'd have to deal with me punching him into a tree.*

James slowed as he approached his dog, who was still mauling the criminal. "You're lucky, asshole. A few inches higher and to the left and you'd have a higher voice," he snapped. "Thomas, come."

The dog released his lock on the man and padded back over to James. He turned to face the mugger and let out a long, low growl.

The woman sat up and gingerly touched the laceration on the side of her head. "God bless you, Mr. Brownstone."

"Brownstone?" the mugger whispered. "But Brownstone don't do anything but level four and up bounties anymore," the man whimpered, clutching his leg. "Everyone knows that."

James glowered at him. "This isn't bounty work, asshole. This is pest control and a workout for my dog. If it wasn't me, it might have been one of my guys. Plenty of them live in this neighborhood, and they wouldn't have been as nice as me." He stared down at the groaning man. "Call the cops right now."

"What?" The mugger blinked.

"Call the fucking cops, asshole." James cracked his knuckles. "Get them here before I decide I could use some exercise, too. It'll be a lot of paperwork if I beat your ass, but if you piss me off enough, I'll pay the price for the stress relief."

The mugger swallowed, then pulled out his phone and dialed 9-1-1. "I'd like to report I just tried to mug someone, and I need cops to come and arrest my ass as soon as possible. No, I'm not fucking lying. I tried to mug this bitch, and

I totally knocked her ass down. I need an ambulance, and she needs an ambulance."

James grinned and crossed his arms. "I think I'm gonna stay until the cops come. Unless you have a fucking problem with that?"

"No, sir." The mugger trembled. "Of course not, sir."

---

*Damn you, Johnston,* thought CIA Agent Karl Nast. *How dare you use the CIA to help you with your damned plans? You haven't won, not yet, and I'll make sure of it.*

Karl glanced around the table at the small group of CIA agents. A few years ago, these men and women represented some of the most elite and best defenses the United States had against non-Oriceran extraterrestrial threats as members of the secret team Fortis. Their group had the direct ear of the President and the authority to do whatever was necessary to protect the country, and now they were reduced to hiding like mobsters on the run. Many of the agents weren't even officially alive anymore.

*Damn everyone who has stood in our way, more concerned about inhuman creatures than the safety of their own country. We've let them humble and humiliate us, and we've been undercut by traitors motivated by naïve idealism. Pretty speeches about morals won't protect this country or planet. The CIA used to understand that.*

"We've been too passive for too long," Karl began. He made eye contact with each agent as he spoke. "It doesn't matter how the situation has changed. Our mission as members of Fortis is to continue to defend this country and planet from aliens, even if the politicians and bureaucrats have allowed themselves to become weak and corrupt." He frowned. "At least with the Oricerans, we have magical parity and linked history, but the events of the last few years have proven again and again that humanity is woefully behind when it comes to alien technology. All the fancy spells in the world will do nothing if the Nine Systems Alliance shows up with some sort of battleship and starts bombarding the planet. Even they are afraid of the Vax, and we've all dealt with other species who possess technology we don't have hard counters for, other than what we've been able to collect from them."

Everyone at the table remained stone-faced. A few nodded.

"I'd hoped the President and the CIA would come to their damned senses given enough time," Karl continued, "but not only have they pulled back on what our mission should be, they have all but given the green light for an invasion by this Nine Systems Alliance. One of their operatives was setting up vast resource chains secretly when she was running around murdering humans." He snorted. "And now it's even worse because I've learned that Company assets are going to be tasked for one of Senator Johnston's new whims, and it's obvious they're trying to make sure we're not involved. We have the right to defend the Earth, and we *will* defend it."

Curiosity rather than irritation covered the face of one of the agents, McKenna. "Are Franklin and Winters and their damned little group of troublemakers going to be involved in Johnston's operation?"

Karl nodded. It was good to know that some of the

others understood just how much trouble Timothy Franklin and Daniel Winters had caused them, even if they were allegedly brother CIA agents. Their little group had gone from being rogues to somehow making Fortis the enemy, despite Franklin and Winters working with hostile aliens.

*Traitors. They should be executed. No, death is too good for them. They've betrayed the country and planet because they're weak. I wish I could use one of those matter transformation guns on them to remind them just who they're dealing with.*

"Yes." Karl slammed his palm on the hard glass surface of the table, raising the eyebrows of a few of the agents. "We've let them poison the CIA and the President, even as they work with all their little foreign mercenaries and Oriceran friends and undermine this country. Fortis has defended this country from hostile threats, and we must continue to do it, even if certain people don't have the stomach for what has to be done. Everything we've done, we've done for the love of country and humanity. If at the end of the day, they want to lock us up and throw away the key, fine, but not before we've purged all alien threats from Earth."

He stood and walked over to a window. The Washington Monument was visible in the distance. It was too easy to forget that such a monument wouldn't last forever. Lines from one of Nast's favorite poems drifted through his thoughts.

*Nothing beside remains: round the decay*
*Of that colossal wreck, boundless and bare,*
*The lone and level sands stretch far away.*

Nothing lasted forever if you didn't have the strength to protect it, and he *would* protect it.

How many tourists were standing near the Monument, and what would happen if an alien ship fired a weapon of mass destruction right at it? Karl doubted people would be overly worried about diplomacy after that. Earth should only negotiate with the aliens from a position of strength.

*This isn't about game or ego, but about protecting the safety of the United States. Are they really going to take away our ability to do that just because a few civilians have been collateral damage now and again? Because we needed to use extraordinary measures to get information from hostile aliens? They accuse us of being the ones trying to start a war when we're trying to stop the war before it ever starts.*

*Aliens aren't people. They are creatures, and they have to be dealt with accordingly.*

Karl narrowed his eyes as he stared at the Monument. The loss of a few lives here and there, or even a town, was a small price to pay. What were hundreds of lives measured against billions?

It was like protecting the body from cancer. Some cells had to die to save the rest.

Agent McKenna frowned. "Agent Nast?"

"We've all made sacrifices," Karl replied, turning back to the table. "Both our fellow agents, and even our fellow citizens. I know that at times, some of you might have questioned those losses. You might find a question arising in the back of your mind if Franklin is right and some of our tactics have been inappropriate or extreme."

A few agents looked down.

*They need to make their decision now. It's not going to get any easier for them. This is our chance to finally take back control of the situation.*

"It's all right to have those questions, but you need to come to the right answers. This is a war." Karl walked back over to his chair and took a seat. "People die in war, including innocent people and children. Sometimes there's no choice if you want to save everyone else. Consider it triage if you must, but make no mistake; we can't pull back now."

The agents nodded slowly, although a few still looked uncomfortable at such a blatant statement confirming the truth of Fortis' harsh tactics.

"This is a war with enemies that share no history or values with us," Karl ranted. "Hostile aliens who fear this planet, so they hide in the shadows, plotting against us in ways the most depraved terrorist would never think of. In war, there is always a sacrifice for the greater good, and we're rapidly approaching a tipping point where the future of this planet will be determined by men and women willing to make the tough choices." He stared down the table, his face grim. "We don't have the resources or personnel we once did, but that doesn't mean we will give up. We will continue to fight, not just for ourselves, but for our country and planet, no matter what the cost."

Agent McKenna snorted. "Franklin and Winters might be the sword, but Johnston's swinging it. That damned old man is as much of a problem as that damned little band of self-righteous rogues."

"Maybe we should assassinate Johnston, then," another agent suggested. "It'll be easy enough to pin it on someone else. I don't understand why we've let him live this long, considering how often he's interfered with us."

Several agents nodded their agreement, no one showing the slightest concern about assassinating a US senator.

Karl shook his head. "The only reason we haven't been crushed totally is that we've shown a certain restraint. There's a tacit understanding here. If we target other members of the CIA or aliens, the politicians can look away and pretend it has nothing to do with them, but if they start dying, they'll be forced to act. But we have an even bigger worry."

"What?" McKenna asked, his brow furrowed.

"That damned alien bounty hunter." Karl's hand curled into a fist.

"Brownstone?"

"Don't give that *thing* the dignity of a human name. It's just an alien pretending to be a man." Karl's face twitched. "He represents the worst-case scenario, long-term infiltration. And it's obvious now that he or others allied with him used significant resources to hide his presence from us until such time as he didn't care, but idiots like Johnston think they can use him. We should have let the Nine Systems Alliance take him. At least we'd have fewer threats."

"You don't buy into Johnston's theory that we can use the alien as a weapon?"

Karl sneered. "A weapon is something you control, not something you have to bargain with. No. If we were lucky, he probably would have ended up killing a lot of the other aliens before they finished him off and we'd be safer overall. Now we still have both threats at full strength."

"Why don't we finish him off ourselves, then?" another agent suggested.

Agent McKenna stared at the man, disbelief on his face. "You're not the first to suggest that. It didn't go well for the Harriken."

"Pathetic gangsters who lacked our training and access to artifacts and technology."

"What about sending him to the World in Between?" Agent McKenna looked at Karl. "It doesn't matter if he's dead, just that he's not on Earth."

Karl scoffed. "This wouldn't be like a normal job. We'd need to gather a large number of magicals, and that's *without* the full resources of the CIA. Purely mercenary wizards might lack the skill to do it, or they'd leak it, and then Franklin and Winters would come after us."

"We should have killed Winters years ago when we first suspected what he was doing," Agent McKenna replied. "Troy Williams should have done his damned job."

"It doesn't matter." Karl narrowed his eyes again. "We have to deal with the future, not the past. I'm not convinced the alien is invincible, especially considering some of the tech we have access to. We're not going to purge the alien influence on Earth by being afraid of aliens. We need to try everything we can, and we do still have a few powerful tools left to us. Besides, the *alien* is one consideration, but Johnston's latest scheme might help us there, too."

"How?"

"From what I've been to able to find out, he's going to

recover some sort of anti-alien weapon, a powerful old magical artifact. If the assassination attempts fail, we can simply use whatever toy Johnston manages to dig up. The first step is to figure out what and where it is. Then we can make sure we get it before Johnston gets his hands on it." Karl surveyed the table, enjoying the belief and confidence displayed on the other agents' faces. "Earth will be safe with Fortis protecting it."

## CHAPTER TWO

Damien Philips, the owner of Philips Bar-B-Que, set a tray of ribs in front of James, a huge smile on his face. "Haven't seen you in a long time, Brownstone. I was beginning to think you hated my place, but then I figured, why would you have paid to have it rebuilt if you hated it?" He pulled some napkins out of his apron and set them on the table.

James looked around at the heavy wooden tables and dark wooden booths. The restaurant looked nothing like the white plastic fest it had been the last time he visited. That wasn't surprising. Getting blasted by Council goons had assured that some redecoration was necessary.

*Those fuckers really picked the wrong place to come at me. Dumbshits. Lucky the fuckers didn't go after my house.*

He pondered that. He'd killed them, so it wasn't clear what worse punishment he could have meted out.

"You need to understand that I don't always have the best luck," James replied.

Damien frowned. "Luck? You're one of the most successful bounty hunters on the planet."

"Yeah, but that shit means people are always coming at me, and that means places like yours get wrecked. So after all that, I decided not to press my luck. You got everything fixed, and I didn't want to walk in here and get your place blown up again because some crazy-ass Oriceran or fucking wizard had a hard-on for trying to kill me. That shit doesn't happen to me nearly as much these days, but I can't guarantee it never will." James shrugged.

"I never thought about it that way." Damien laughed. "That makes sense. I know this sounds twisted as hell, but my place getting blasted by those guys was the best thing that ever happened to my business."

"Huh?"

"You see, I was just kind of getting by, but now I'm raking in the dough. At the rate things are going, I might even be able to open up a second place soon. Not sure if I'm going to call it Philips Bar-B-Que Two or something else."

James sampled a rib, taking a few bites. Good sauce work. There was a reason he used to hit the place regularly. "How does that work? Somebody come in and invest?"

"Nope, just better business. Lots more pick-up orders and foot traffic. It didn't cost me anything to rebuild, thanks to you." Damien pulled out a chair and took a seat across from James. "And because the attack was related to the Council, I got a lot of publicity. All sorts of news types wanted interviews about the attack, about you. Hell, about barbeque." He gestured to the ribs. "Turns out they're right."

"'They?' Who is 'they?'"

"You know, 'they.'" Damien made air quotes. "The *they* who always say shit like, 'There is no such thing as bad publicity.' I always thought people would be too afraid to come, but I was wrong. Once my place reopened, tons of people wanted to come to the restaurant where Brownstone took those bad guys down. A lot of barbeque people figured if *you* were a customer here, there was a good reason."

James grunted. "True enough. I was coming here because I liked the barbeque." He held up a rib. "I still do. Sorry I made you think I hated it."

"No problem. The important thing is that you're here now." Damien pointed to a picture across the room. "I've even got a photo of the burned-out old place next to the picture I have of you on the wall. I think this is what they call creative destruction. It sucked at the time, but I've got no problems with how things went down now."

James chuckled. "You're a much better businessman than I am. I would have just been pissed and kicked ass until I felt better. Fuck, I *was* pissed at the time, and I *did* kick ass."

"You're the reason this is happening, though. You even paid my staff's wages during the construction. I still don't know how I can thank you. If it wasn't for you, I'd have been so screwed and so would they, thanks to my worthless insurance company." Damien snorted. "I got a new one. Don't know if they'll be better in that situation. We'll just have to see, the next time I get blown up. So thanks for all your help."

"It was my fault your place got fucked up, and I clean up

my messes. Simple as that." James shrugged. "You've got nothing to thank me for. I'd be pissed at me if I was you. I brought you a lot of shit, and you had to deal with the aftermath. That wasn't fair."

"I'm not pissed, I'm grateful. Let me make that clear." Damien shook his head. "It doesn't sit right with me that I haven't paid you back somehow. Can I at least offer you free food when you come? Like the ribs you're eating?"

"No. I pay for what I eat." James grunted. "If you want to do anything, you can offer a discount to my guys. I'll let them know, but don't let any of those fuckers try to con you out of free ribs. I don't want Brownstone Agency employees running around freeloading."

"In other words, more business for me." Damien looked thoughtful. "Can't say I don't like the sound of it. Not a bad deal at all."

"Yeah, and a lot of them are on our barbeque team, too, so it'll help for them to sample high-quality barbeque. Also, having Brownstone Agency guys coming here regularly who aren't me will probably cut down on the chance of petty robbery. The big guys like the Council come after me, not my guys." James frowned. "Well, usually, but I can't make any guarantees."

Damien waved a hand. "I'm sure it'll be fine. I'd love to have your guys."

It wasn't as if he needed the business. Every table and booth was filled, the occasional person lifting their phone to take a picture of James.

Several people had already come and asked for autographs, but he had made it clear that once his food had arrived, people were to leave him the fuck alone, other than pictures. He didn't get the appeal of some random phone picture of him, but it didn't hurt him, either.

*This barbeque was great even before the place got wrecked, but he said his business sucked. Flavor isn't everything, huh?*

"Did you always want to have your own barbeque place?" James asked. "Is this like a family deal or something?"

He felt bad for never asking before, but he tended to care about taste first and everything else a far distant second.

"No, not a family deal. Everyone I knew said I was a damned fool for opening a barbeque place. My family was the loudest about that." Damien folded his arms as he pondered the question. "I was an accountant before opening this place." He laughed. "I worked in a big fancy auditing firm for a while. I can't complain about it. My bosses weren't dicks, and I made good money. It was a good, steady job. Easy in its own way."

"How did you end up doing barbeque then?" James watched a woman take a bite out of a brisket sandwich.

"I always liked cooking barbeque, but I always figured owning a restaurant wasn't a stable career path, and like I said, everyone I knew kept telling me that, too. It's hard to swim against the current when no other fish is even trying." Damien nodded to a couple in a booth gobbling down ribs. "But I asked myself at one point, 'When am I happiest?' And the answer was always the same. I was happiest when I was cooking barbeque for people. It wasn't like I hated my old job, but when that time hit where I was questioning choices, midlife crisis or whatever you want to call it, I decided to open a restaurant instead of buying a sports car." He chuckled.

James finished off another rib. "Do you ever regret it? Ever think you should go back to your old job?"

"No, not for a second." Damien shrugged. "Every day, I think I made the right choice. I make good food that people like, and I'm doing something I like. Sure, margins were tight at first, and I could have made more money at my old job, but there's something to be said for doing what you love. And now everything's going my way. I just needed to hang in there."

James considered the man's story. Unlike Damien, the bounty hunter had millions of dollars in savings and a successful business that no longer required his direct involvement. Financial considerations weren't relevant if he decided to open a place. He could operate at a loss until the day he died if he wanted.

But he didn't want to do that. If he was going to open a restaurant, doing anything less than striving for success was pointless. He already cooked as a hobby, but running an actual restaurant should be different. If he ran it like a hobby, it'd never be successful.

"Must feel good, seeing all these people enjoying something you made." James stared down at the ribs on his plate as he pondered the balance of spices in the sauce. "When you're a bounty hunter, a lot of people aren't happy when you're doing your job." He chuckled. "Other than the cops, but it's not like they've ever been happy to see me when I have shown up at a bounty's house."

"I can imagine." Damien laughed. "Why? You thinking

about quitting the bounty hunting game and opening a barbeque restaurant?"

"Yeah, actually." James looked up.

Damien's smile fell away, and he swallowed. "Seriously?"

"I've thought about it. Never gonna quit all the way, but because of the Brownstone Agency, I've got a lot more free time. And my kid goes to boarding school, so I don't see her most of the year. I've been doing a lot with my barbeque team, but opening my own place is the natural next step."

Damien nodded slowly as he paled even more. "Sure. We could always use more people in the barbeque game, but please, I'm begging you—don't open your place near mine. You're starting out with freaking Hollywood-level name recognition. You'll dominate whatever neighborhood you open your place, and every place around you will get destroyed."

James grunted. "It'll be a while before I open a place, but sure. I'm not interested in fucking over anyone else. I'll check around. That's assuming I even do. Not sure if it's just bullshit running through my head."

Some color returned to Damien's face, and he let out a sigh of relief. "I always figured you liked taking down bounties. You know, that it was fun."

"Sometimes. It's satisfying to take down assholes like that mind-control fucker a few months back, but sometimes I'd rather just spend a week concentrating on experimenting with sauces instead of tracking down some asshole." James nodded toward the window. "And there are fewer and fewer high-level bounties showing up in LA anyway. The roaches are all hiding somewhere else these days. They've learned their lesson."

There *was* such a thing as being too good at your job.

"You could travel around," Damien suggested. "I remember that big bounty you took down in Detroit. There is always garbage somewhere in the country, let alone elsewhere in the world. Maybe you could go around to every headquarters of all the different mobs and take them out."

James shook his head. "I don't want shit to get complicated, and my fiancée just got a permanent position at UCLA. I need to keep my life a little more stable."

"Really?" Damien asked. "Congrats. I see your dilemma. You heard what I just said. I think running a barbeque place is great, and I think you'd be great at it, too, as long you build it far, far away from my place." He stood and extended his hand. "I better get back in the kitchen before my staff decides to barbeque *me*. Thanks again for everything you've done for me, Brownstone."

James gave the man's hand a firm shake. "No problem."

Damien headed back into the kitchen.

*I could do it. The way things are going, it won't be long until I only see a level four or higher every six months in LA. That could be the side job, and I could spend the next fifty years experimenting until I made something even better than God Sauce.*

*Shit. Don't know if that's even possible.*

---

James stared at Shay as she finished explaining an unusual punishment she'd doled out to a student. They'd been chatting about her day in the living room. Listening to her discuss dealing with college students instead of putting bullets in some mercenary's head was still strange at times. He wasn't sure if he was completely comfortable with the transition.

"Wait," he responded as he processed what she had just told him. "So you're saying this kid thinks he's haunted now?"

Shay laughed. "Yeah. Once I realized the little sonofabitch was plagiarizing, I thought about how I should handle it. The easy thing would have been to go to the department and initiate a big, annoying formal process to get him in trouble, but I figured, in the spirit of second chances, I'd do something different to scare him straight." She rolled her eyes. "Reminds me of Peyton's brother. Too bad that shit didn't work on him. It would have saved everyone a lot of trouble. But some people can't learn, no matter how hard you try to teach them."

"I don't get it. How the fuck did you make some random college kid think he was haunted?" James thought the whole thing was too complicated. His solution would have been to throw the plagiarist through a window. Universities would probably frown on his straightforward Brownstone Anti-Plagiarism Method, simple and efficient as it was.

Thomas stood up from where he'd been lying and moved to the couch by Shay. He circled a few times before sitting down in front of her and cocking his head to the side to watch her.

"Peyton's been a little bored for the last few weeks anyway, so I recruited him for a little fun." Shay leaned over to scratch behind Thomas' ears. "He hacked the student's computer and sent him spooky messages and a few old pictures of some random professor-looking guy we grabbed off the web. The messages claimed to be from the spirit of a professor who died right after the gates began opening and was trapped between worlds. He now haunts students who don't do their own work in a feeble attempt to find rest." She snickered. "And this idiot bought it. He actually came to me and begged me to allow him to turn in a new version of the paper. Said he'd misunderstood some things."

James snorted. "What a dumbass."

"I told him fine." Shay offered an evil smile. "And then I lied about seeing someone in the doorway who looked like our fake professor. When the student turned around, I was all, 'Shit. He just disappeared. That's magic for you.' I swear that little fucker was ready to wet himself right then and there." She snickered.

"He'll probably call the PDA or AET eventually."

"I hope he does. That'll be extra fun." A thoughtful expression crossed Shay's face. "I had another department meeting today. I'll spare you the boring details, but I think I'll need to do some occasional field work. They don't mind having me as only a lecturer now, but that won't last forever."

Thomas curled up beside Shay's feet, ready for a nap.

"Isn't archaeology field work just tomb raiding without killing anyone?" James suggested with a curious expression.

"Sort of. I've done that shit before. Remember when that CIA guy had me doing normal recovery jobs for him?

Sure, they were artifact-recovery-focused rather than general archaeology, but it was the same basic idea."

James grunted. "You told me you ended up taking some people down anyway on the big job you did for him."

"Yeah." Shay grinned. "But I wasn't hired to do that. The guy didn't seem eager to hire me again once he realized I was a tomb raider and not just a brave archaeologist, though. Funny thing, too, considering he went to the trouble of helping me. Or maybe…"

"Maybe?"

Shay's mouth contorted into a frown. "The guy was into aliens. If he realized what you were, he might have wanted to stay the fuck away. Despite some of the lines he gave me about his goals, it might have been that he was just as into handling things in a black ops sort of way as what I was seeing from the assholes associated with Projects Nephilim and Ragnarök. Not gonna bitch too much about being ghosted by a CIA agent, but it's still a little annoying."

"It's good he left you alone."

"Oh?"

James nodded. "Yeah. Fuck working for the government, anyway, especially some spy. If he really cared about half the shit he told you about, he would have been doing more than grabbing artifacts in random countries. Not being a complete dick isn't the same thing as being trustworthy. The guy lies all the time for his job. For all you know, he's killed tons of people who were just in the wrong place at the wrong time."

"I know, but it was still kind of strange how it went down." Shay looked at Thomas for a moment. "And I doubt he's a total piece of shit. I can't say the guy screwed me or anything. He paid me for what I did, and he helped me with Yulia. The ghosting was kind of annoying, but he's CIA. But you're right. That's kind of what they do; I knew what I was getting into. He's not important anyway. The important thing is that I'm going to have to go on some digs. Given my specialties, I might end up going to more dangerous places than a lot of my colleagues."

James grunted. "If you kill a bunch of monsters or bandits or whatever, won't people get suspicious?"

He wasn't sure how necessary it was for Shay to hide her true history, but she had put a lot of effort into keeping her background from most people, so she obviously felt there was still value in keeping it concealed.

*I've been hiding shit, too. I confess to Father McCartney, but he doesn't know what I am. I don't know if that's okay or not, but it also might not be safe for him to know. It's not like being an alien is a sin, and the sins are what I'm being forgiven for. Lying to a priest has to be a sin, though, even by omission.*

Shay pointed at James, pulling him out of his theological thoughts. "You can solve that problem. You're convenient that way."

"Huh? Convenient?" James grimaced. "I don't want to go on archaeology digs. They sound boring as fuck. Sitting around digging all day? Come on. You think I'd actually like that?"

There was no reason to lie about the truth. It wasn't like he'd kept his preferences hidden in the past, and if they were going to get married, all the more reason to be honest. Besides, he *really* didn't want to have to go on boring digs.

"Your lack of love for ancient history and knowledge is

forever a dark spot against you, James Brownstone." Shay shook a finger at him. "But I'm not talking about bringing you along on digs. You'd probably blow up all the artifacts. I'm talking about the fact that everyone knows I'm dating you. If I go on a dig and end up having to kick someone's ass, I can just say, 'Oh, well, James taught me that because he was worried about some criminal kidnapping me,' and everyone will nod like it's the most obvious thing in the world. You're a convenient excuse in a lot of ways for anything that seems weird or off about my life."

"Oh." James grunted. "I guess that shit will work. You going on a dig anytime soon?"

Shay shook her head. "Probably in the summer, but I'll make sure I hang out with Alison at least some of the time during the break." A wistful expression took over her face. "A few years back I was plotting how to escape a murderous cartel and planning to disappear forever. Now I'm working a semi-normal job and worrying about spending time with a teenager who is soon to be my daughter. I didn't see *that* shit coming. You change people by being around them, James. You're kind of a hurricane that wrecks things but leaves them better after the storm passes."

"I'm the same man I always was." James shrugged. "I haven't changed shit about other people."

"The only bigger lie than that would be if you said you hate barbeque."

James grunted. "Need a hundred of those mind-control artifacts to get me to say *that* shit."

"Probably a thousand. Ten thousand." Shay tilted her head, her gaze focused on his chest. "You busy tomorrow?"

"I've got a PFW meeting in the afternoon, but that's it. Why?"

Shay pointed at his chest. "I was reading something the other day about the gates and magic levels, and it got me thinking about that shit in Romania and some of the stuff with Whispy."

"What about it?"

"You haven't been able to reach advanced mode without getting pissed pretty much since then. I thought he said he was modifying you so you wouldn't need to. You know, use all the background magic and shit?"

"I think he's tried his best, but there are limits." James reached under his shirt and fingered the amulet. "From what he says, there's not enough magic outside of weird places like that forest or kemanas for the adaptation to work by itself. Maybe in a few hundred years. I'll probably be dead long before then, though."

"I see." Shay nodded slowly. "In that case, I've got some ideas. Let's hit Warehouse Five tomorrow and do some more tests."

## CHAPTER THREE

S hay's 9mm bullets bounced off James' chest and clattered on the cement floor of the warehouse, as crumpled from the force of impact as if she'd been shooting them into a thick metal wall. She gave up after ten shots and pulled off her ear protection.

"It's a shame to even try to harm those abs," she murmured. She'd told James to take off his shirt, since there was no reason to destroy a perfectly good shirt with their experiments. Tendrils from his already-bonded amulet visibly extended into much of his upper chest, and the amulet had sunken in, as it normally did.

James used to be slightly embarrassed when Shay saw him this way, but she never seemed to care or mind. She couldn't hear the symbiont, and in some ways, she still treated Whispy as a fancy artifact rather than the intelligent, self-aware entity he was. For now, that made everything better for all three of them.

*Recommend varied attacks for greater adaptation,* Whispy sent. He'd made the same complaint concerning the previous few attacks from Shay: a knife, a tube that blasted fireballs, and a vial of acid.

*It's fine. We'll get to something interesting. Shay knows what she's doing.*

After what had happened in Romania, James was more grateful than ever about how thorough Shay had been in helping the symbiont's adaptation range. He wasn't sure he would have escaped as unscathed as he had from some of the encounters in the forest without that previous exposure to many attack types. It was easy to anticipate that an enemy might use a fireball or bullet, but in a world of magic, monsters and alien nanoforms, a little extra training and lateral thinking could save a man's life.

*Maybe she's got a special artifact she wants to try, and she just wants to make sure everything's the same as it was before the forest.*

Weapons and artifacts filled several nearby tables. So far, none of the tests had done more than scratch or tickle James.

Shay furrowed her brow and grabbed her *tachi* from a table. "Might as well establish more baselines just to be sure." She looked uncertain as she flexed her fingers around the hilt of the long blade.

"It can't hurt me anymore. That Harriken bastard got one chance, and he fucked it up." James made a fist and raised his arm. "Go ahead." He grunted. "Even if you chop it off, I should be able to use Whispy combined with a potion to regenerate it. Might be good to practice. Almost have to thank He Who Hunts for helping me learn that."

"Yeah, what a helpful guy. Thing. Whatever the fuck he was, and no, we're *not* going to practice regenerating lost limbs, since lost limbs are a lot more than regenerating lost fingers, which is what happened last time." Shay swung the sword, which bounced off James' arm with a clang and left only a shallow scratch. With more confidence in her movements, she stabbed at his chest, but the second blow didn't hurt him any worse than the first attack. A third slash also proved pointless.

*Ineffective attacks for adaptation,* Whispy complained. *Near maximum adaptation achieved.*

*Get over it. We're trying some shit here. We can't get stronger if we don't know our limits.*

"Huh," Shay murmured. "I just realized something."

"What?" James asked.

Shay set the sword down and walked over to tap the amulet. "You're tougher now even without advanced mode armor. A lot tougher. It used to be at least I could get a half-decent cut in with some of this stuff, but now I can't even scratch you after simple bonding, and that's before we even start talking about your way more powerful regeneration."

"Yeah, well, he's been tinkering and shit." James shrugged. "Optimizing me. There are some tradeoffs, but he's doing the stuff that works best with the way I fight."

Shay tilted her head as she looked James up and down. "Does that ever bother you?"

"Not anymore." James patted the amulet. "I'm not even human, and he basically made me human. He fucked with my genes and shit from the very beginning. It's too late to start bitching now. He's had plenty of time to make changes that I didn't want, but he hasn't, other than that shit when I was a kid. If he fucks with me too much, he knows I'll just never put him on again or throw him in a volcano or some shit."

*Continued usage necessary for maximum adaptation,* Whispy noted.

*Yeah, yeah, yeah. Just keep in mind what might happen if you don't do what I say.*

Shay laughed. "For a guy who wants to keep his life simple, accepting that an amulet has rewritten your DNA and continues to do so seems a bit much."

"How is it complicated? It's not like I have to do anything," James replied. "Do you spend a lot of time thinking about how your cells work in your body?"

"No, I suppose I don't. True enough. Anyway, let's get back to business and do another baseline test." Shay smiled as she slid her ear protection back on, walked over to another table, and picked up a high-powered rifle. "A little muzzle velocity makes all the difference to normal people." She aimed it at his shoulder and pulled the trigger.

The loud crack echoed throughout the warehouse as the bullet bounced off his shoulder, leaving a small scratch that started to heal after a few seconds. James wasn't bothering to wear anything to protect his hearing, but the loud noises weren't hurting his ears. Another example of adaptation.

*You can become the perfect weapon if you let go long enough for him to change you. Does that mean the Vax normally don't?*

"I adapt," James noted. "I've always adapted to shit. I used to think it was just him adapting, but now I get it's always been both of us. So, no, it doesn't freak me out, because it's useful."

"But you've adapted a lot more these last few years than

the rest of your life." Shay set the rifle down. "I wonder why that is? Why the acceleration? I know you've been using him more, but I think it's more than just that."

*Maximum link integration necessary for extended modification without risk of neural damage. Improved link integration facilitating more efficient adaptation.*

James chuckled. "If I'm understanding him, it's because I can talk to him now."

"That makes sense, as much as anything with adaptative alien symbionts make sense. The question becomes how much that extends out. You've got to have some sort of limit."

James grunted. "Yeah, anti-matter torpedoes."

"Very funny. But seriously, if we exposed you to enough radiation and explosions, would you be able to survive a nuke?" Shay eyed him as if she had one in a backroom she wanted to try out.

*She doesn't have a nuke, does she?*

James made a face. "Yeah, well, some shit, I don't want to test."

"Don't tempt me." Shay picked up a wavy jet-black dagger off the table, an Indonesian *kris*, and walked forward, weapon in hand. "This isn't a nuke, but it might be fun to try. I picked this up as a bonus on a tomb raid. It's magical, but since my gnome knives and the *tachi* no longer seem to hurt you, I wanted to see if something else magical might. If it doesn't work, I've got another idea."

*Engage in further exposure for maximum adaptation,* Whispy demanded.

*You mean the knife or the nuke?*

*Engage in further exposure to all adaptation potential that won't result in unit termination.*

James snorted. *So, what...the edge of a nuke explosion?*

*Maximum adaptation necessary to achieve primary directive. Strategic-scale weaponry exposure necessary for maximum adaptation.*

Shay frowned. "What's wrong?"

"Nothing. Whispy's just got delusions of grandeur." James held out his arm. "Do it."

Shay slashed at the arm, but the blade bounced off as if she had tried to cut through solid metal. A thin scratch was the only thing he earned for her efforts.

"Too similar to the other shit, even if it is magic," James suggested. "I mean, even magic's got to be kind of like regular forces, with some of it related, right? It can't all be unique. If it was, the Oricerans wouldn't be able to counter each other."

"True enough, and there is enough similarity that they can teach all sorts of different types of magicals at the School of Necessary Magic," Shay suggested.

James grunted. "What was your other idea?"

Shay held out the *kris* handle-first. "If Whispy has adapted to power himself off magic but there's not enough background magic in most places on Earth for it to work, why not just use a battery as a jumpstart?"

"A battery?" James took the knife. "Like in a kemana?"

"That's a possibility, but it's not like you can stop in the middle of a fight and say, 'Excuse me, I need to go to a semi-hidden magic town and charge up. Be right back.'" Shay nodded at the knife. "But if you could somehow take the magic from an artifact, that might be useful. Sometimes you might want to be revved up before shit gets really bad, and if this works, you don't have to be so pissed, and you could focus more on a fight." She reached into her pocket and pulled out a healing potion. "Before we try that though, let's see if this works." She held out the vial. "This would be more cost-effective, as expensive as these are."

James took the vial, offering Shay a confused look. "We already know healing potions work. We know Whispy can combine them with his power already. Shit, we already kind of talked about that earlier."

"You're not understanding my point. It's magical. He might be able to take the magic from it to fuel a transformation. If it works, it'll end up being more practical than my other idea, because I have some theories on what's going to happen if you try to take the magic from the knife. This is one of the potions that was specifically brewed to work for you."

James eyed the potion for a moment. "It's worth a try."

"Exactly. Let's see what you've got."

*Try to take the magic from this for power.*

James downed the potion, and the harsh, unpleasant flavor coated his tongue. He wasn't hurt, so there was no way to judge if the potion was doing anything, and he didn't feel any different.

*Hey, let's go to advanced mode,* he thought.

*Power insufficient for advanced transformation,* Whispy responded.

*Can't you take it from the potion?*

*Insufficient matrix capability for alternate power source usage.*

*Can you adapt or some shit to make it possible?*

*Necessary baseline matrix modifications would result in unacceptable reduction of tactical potential.*

James wasn't surprised, but that didn't keep him from being disappointed.

Shay had been wrong to ask if James had limits. Whispy had already related that he did. There had been countless small trade-offs as the host and symbiont had adapted to each other, including the sacrifice of certain abilities. That didn't mean he wouldn't be a terrifying weapon, just that there would always be some small weakness that a clever enemy might potentially exploit.

James shook his head. "It didn't work. From what Whispy was saying, I don't think it will work with potions without fucking up a bunch of other stuff." He shrugged.

"But between what you remembered and what the Alliance has said, you're probably nowhere near your full potential," Shay responded. "I don't get it. If it only takes a small number of Vax to invade a planet, that means a full-powered Vax has got to be equivalent to thousands or tens of thousands of troops, and they have to be able to survive anything short of city-destroying attacks. You're tough, James, but I don't think you're that tough…yet."

"And you want me to get that tough?"

"I think it'd be nice to have it in our back pocket, yeah." Shay furrowed her brow.

"You're thinking like a human," James replied.

Shay laughed. "Well, I *am* human as far as I know, but what do you mean?"

James pointed at the amulet. "The Vax don't care if the host is full of rage and out of control. The symbiont encourages it because the host is just supposed to supply the energy while the symbiont controls everything else. They probably never worried about sending a Forerunner who was calm to fuck shit up, so they never needed to work out alternate power sources." He shrugged again. "They're supposed to show up and kill everybody in sight, and being bloodthirsty and full of anger only would just make that easier."

"That makes sense. It's like complaining that your truck doesn't work if I pour sugar in the gas tank instead of gas, even if it *is* an energy source. It's just not something that was part of the original design." Shay frowned. "The potion thing was worth a shot." She pointed to the *kris*. "Let's try that now."

"How exactly? I can't stab myself with it." James eyed the dagger. *Can you take the magic from this, Whispy?*

*Potential matrix capability for alternate power source. Insufficient contact.*

*Insufficient contact?* James placed the blade against the amulet at the center of his chest. *How about now?*

*Matrix capability established, initiating use of alternate power source. Adaptation in progress.*

"Is it working?" Shay asked, her eyes narrowed in concentration.

James nodded slowly "Not sure, but I think so."

The *kris* glowed brightly for a few seconds.

*Initiating advanced transformation.*

Silver-green metallic tendrils shot from the amulet and coalesced into armor around James' arms, legs, and chest. The transformation shredded his pants. He dropped the *kris* as the transformation began. A large, sharp blade extended from the top of his right arm.

Shay clapped and whistled. "Perfect. Fucking perfect. How do you feel? Pissed or normal, which is just slightly less pissed?"

"I'm not always pissed," James rumbled. "People are just fucking annoying. That's their fault, not mine."

"I'll keep that in mind."

He stared down at the armor covering his limbs. Although he'd managed to achieve advanced transformation in situations without all-consuming rage before, this was the first time he'd ever done so while completely calm. It allowed him to take in the small details such as the whorls covering the mottled armor.

"I feel fine." James shrugged. "Don't feel angry at all. Wait one second; let me check on something."

*If I'm not pissed, does that mean I'm going to run out of power if I have to fight?*

*Advanced transformation allows more efficient harvesting of background alternative energy for power,* Whispy responded. *Warning: enhanced emotional state necessary for maximum efficiency.*

"If I'm understanding him right," James rumbled, "once I transform I'll be able to maintain it, but I'll be tougher if I get more pissed."

Shay slowly circled him, eyeing the armor. "This is a good start, then." She picked up the knife and handed it to him. "See if you can get anything else out of it."

James placed the dagger against his chest again.

*Object no longer possesses alternate power potential,* Whispy sent.

James shook his head. "I think it's permanently drained."

"Good to know. Too bad we can't get the potions to work, but I can at least collect a lot of minor artifacts to jumpstart you." Shay laughed. "The problem is that you're getting less and less pissed at shit as the months pass, even when you're on jobs."

James shrugged. "Got fewer reasons to be pissed, and even a lot of bounty assholes are getting smarter about fucking with me."

"Not saying it's a bad thing. It's just, sometimes we might need more than basic-level ass-kicking from you when you're not pissed off." Shay ran her hand over the armor. "Huh. It's not as smooth as it looks." She headed over to another table and pointed at a nearby wall. "Now that you've got that on, let's test something else." She continued walking and picked up a curled horn. "Ready?"

"I don't even know what the fuck that does."

Shay laughed. "Nothing you haven't been exposed to before, just a higher power level. I got this a few jobs back and forgot to mention it to you. Have Whispy try to take power from it as I blast you."

"Fine." James squared his shoulders. "Do it."

Shay pointed the horn at his chest and intoned an incantation in Old Persian.

The entire room shook.

*Moderate potential for adaptation,* Whispy announced, a hint of excitement leaking from the symbiont. *Achieve maximum adaptation for primary directive.*

A massive bolt of lightning blasted from the horn and struck James, blinding him. He stumbled back a few feet, but he didn't feel anything other than mild tingles as electricity arced over his body.

*Near maximum adaptation previously achieved,* Whispy griped. *Human female's actions are inefficient. Exposure to new sources necessary for maximum adaptation.*

The horn crumbled into dust that floated to the ground.

Shay dusted her hands. "Okay, that was an expensive-ass test, and you're barely scorched. Did he take anything from it?" She looked hopeful.

*Did you?* James sent.

*Immediate defensive reaction not compatible with energy harvesting from alternate power source.*

"Nope. He can't protect me and harvest shit at the same time."

Shay frowned. "Damn. Well, it was worth a shot. Probably should call it for today. At least we figured out something that might help."

## CHAPTER FOUR

James changed lanes on his way to the pet store, in a good mood as he thought about what they'd accomplished at the warehouse the day before. Shay's experiments had provided the potential for more tactical flexibility. He might not be using Whispy as much in recent months, but when he did need the symbiont, his enemies were a little tougher than average.

*Even I can't be pissed all the time, so whatever works.*

"The real challenge," explained a podcast host, "is getting used to the meat temperatures."

The barbeque podcast he was listening to was focusing on an unusual and underserved topic: traditional barbeque techniques applied to meat from Oriceran animals. The heavy restrictions on legally bringing animals over from the other planet had limited any real alternative meat scene from arising, but that didn't make James less curious. He might have to take a trip over to the other planet for a research mission.

*The only time I've gone was to kick ass. There's a lot of potential there.*

James chuckled.

*I spent all that time listening to relationship and wedding podcasts, but I haven't listened to one in months since it's all in Shay's hands now. I wonder if she's listening to podcasts now about wedding planning while I'm enjoying thinking about all the delicious Oriceran animals I might eat in the future.*

James' phone rang with a call from an unknown number. He answered it on speakerphone. "Yeah?"

"This is James Brownstone, correct?" came a deep male voice over the line. It had a slight accent James couldn't place. Maybe central European?

*Shit. This better not be someone who is going to ruin my fucking mood.*

"What about it?" James rumbled. "Who the fuck is this?"

"I was…a friend of Erin North, I suppose you could say," the man replied. "It's a shame she disappeared. Even more of a shame what she became."

*Yeah, Shay. Don't need any extra power now.*

James growled. "Is this line secure?"

"Yes, why?"

"Because I need to make sure about some shit before I get pissed off."

The man chuckled. "Oh? I didn't realize you were so easy to irritate."

"Being friends with a woman who tried to kill me and hurt my friends is one way to set me off," James replied.

The man sighed. "Understandable."

"Yeah." James waited for his chance and performed a hard U-turn, his truck shaking. He couldn't take the chance of a showdown at the pet store again. He liked that pet store, and Thomas loved the groomers there.

*Fucking aliens. Don't mess with me on the way to the damned pet store. Make a goddamn appointment or whatever.*

"What is it that you needed to be sure of?" the man asked.

James checked his mirrors for drones. There were a few delivery drones flying nearby and a traffic drone in the distance, but nothing that appeared to be following him. There were also no odd light patterns to suggest a hidden alien ship.

"I wanted to make sure you're with the Nine Systems Alliance," James explained.

"Ah. Yes, I am. I understand your concern about secure lines now. I should have made that clear from the outset."

James grunted. "I'm not in the mood for bullshit or games. What's this about, alien boy? Looking for vengeance?"

"I just want to talk, Mr. Brownstone. I assure you of that. I understand that due to your experiences in the past with the Alliance, you might be ill-inclined to trust me. However, we both know that if I wanted to attack you, I have many means available, and there's no reason for me to warn you ahead of time."

"That supposed to be a threat?" James' hands tightened on the wheel.

"No, more of an explanation." The man sighed. "So, what will it be? Aren't you the least bit curious?"

James gritted his teeth. He didn't want to deal with anything annoying and alien that wasn't Whispy Doom, but he needed to find out what the man wanted. If aliens were going to start coming after him and his people again, he had to be prepared.

"I'm assuming you know where I live?" James asked.

"Yes. Why?"

"Come there, and we'll talk," James replied.

"You're inviting me to your house?" The man sounded incredulous.

"What can I say? I've got some leftover brisket."

"Very well, then." A slight chuckle followed. "How about I come in two hours?"

"Fine by me."

*I just invited the enemy to my house. If that fucker blows it up, I'm personally declaring war on the Nine Systems Alliance.*

James waited, his arms folded, on his front porch, wearing one of his ugly gray coats. He'd armed up and already bonded Whispy, but he hadn't contacted Shay. He didn't want her rushing across town. If it turned into a fight against the alien, he'd need to go all-out to win, and if it didn't, coming home would be a waste of Shay's time.

A black electric Lexus pulled into the driveway, and a handsome brown-haired man in a dark suit stepped out. He offered James a polite nod before he walked to the porch.

*He looks just like anyone else. At least I have the fucking decency to have a messed-up face and shit.*

James stepped inside and waited for the visitor to follow. The man entered and closed the door behind him. He lowered his hand toward a silver bracelet.

The bounty hunter whipped out a .45 and pointed it at his head. "You try anything and I put a bullet in your head, asshole."

*High adaptation potential,* Whispy announced. *Engage and kill enemy for maximum adaptation.*

*That's on him.*

*Engage and kill enemy.*

The man arched an eyebrow. "Touchy, aren't we?"

"You don't know the half of it." James snorted. "The last two Alliance people I dealt with either kept trying to kill me or threatened to kill me, so I've got no fucking reason at all to trust any of you people."

The man nodded slowly. "I was going to make sure our conversation is private. Although I'm sure you've also taken measures, I prefer to use my own. After all, we both know your government likes to keep an eye on you, Mr. Brownstone."

James grunted. "Fine. I'll keep my gun up until I make sure you didn't just call in an airstrike."

The man laughed and tapped his bracelet. There was a slight shift in the air, with the area growing quieter.

James waited ten seconds and slowly lowered his gun. "Just so you know, if you're feeling brave, I've already bonded my symbiont, and I've fought nanites multiple times. I'm fully adapted to several different types of energy they can generate and a bunch of other fancy Alliance shit."

The man's face twitched. "I see." He stared at James' coat. "It's beneath there, isn't it? You have to understand how fascinating this is to me. A free Vax Forerunner is... almost an oxymoron. I'm not going to claim we understand everything about the Vax, but we've learned a lot."

"I really don't give a shit about what the Nine Systems Alliance thinks or knows. It's got nothing to do with Earth or me." James holstered his gun and headed toward his kitchen. "You want some brisket?"

The man laughed. "You were serious about that?"

"If there's one thing I'm always serious about, it's fucking barbeque." James opened his refrigerator and removed a foil-wrapped plate. "Reheating it isn't the best, but it's still decent."

"I'm fine." The man waved a hand. "I ate before I came here."

James eyed him with suspicion, wondering what the man ate. From what Shay had said, Erin could eat human food, but maybe that was some sort of nanite trick.

"Fine." James put the plate back in the refrigerator and closed the door. He pointed to the dining room table before heading in there to take a seat. "So who the fuck are you anyway, other than an alien with a death wish?"

"Alien?" the man replied before taking his own seat. "That's an odd term when you think about it, considering the bizarre magical species you have running all over this planet. Aren't they just as alien?"

James shrugged. "Don't really give a fuck. To me, an alien is someone who comes from outer space. Oricerans come from Oriceran. Foreigners come from other countries. Simple shit."

The man gave him a tight smile. "You came from outer space originally too, Mr. Brownstone."

"Yes, and I'm not going to ask again." James glared at him. "Who the fuck are you?"

"Sentry 8224, Senior Shepherd Corayailaxi Jakimalitta."

Several of the syllables in his names contained odd clicking that didn't sound like something a normal humanoid could make.

"That's a fucking mouthful. It must suck when people have to sing you *Happy Birthday*."

The Shepherd smiled. "On Earth, I go by Corey Jakima."

James nodded, looking him up and down. "You also a Smurf?"

Corey's smile faded. "A Smurf? I'm afraid I'm not following you, Mr. Brownstone."

"Blue people, like Erin North's true form."

Understanding spread across the alien's face. "I see. No, I'm not a…Smurf, as you call it. I'm a different species, but I assure you I represent the Nine Systems Alliance's interests on Earth. We want to see how those interests might coincide or oppose those of the Vax on the Earth, and that's what I'm here to discuss today."

James growled. "I don't represent the Vax on Earth or their fucking interests."

*Engage and kill enemy,* Whispy demanded. *Achieve maximum adaptation.*

*Shut it. I don't want to fight this guy in my neighborhood.*

James gritted his teeth. He might have made a mistake in bringing the Shepherd to his house instead of meeting him in the middle of nowhere, like maybe the Salton Sea.

Corey folded his hands in front of him. "You're wearing a Vax symbiont. Even if you don't want to serve their interests, you're doing just that by bonding that thing."

"You don't know shit about me. You grew up on some planet far away. I grew up here. I go to church here. I'm getting married to a human woman. I know what the fuck a Smurf is."

"Yes, I'm aware of all those fascinating contradictions and facts." Corey stared at him. "The thing you've admitted to wearing doesn't care about any of that. It only cares about death and killing, and don't try to lie to me and tell me it doesn't. It's rare for us to have captured a Vax, but it's not unprecedented. We've gained valuable intel from them."

*Engage and kill enemy,* Whispy sent on cue.

James shrugged. "I'm the one calling the shots here, not him, so it doesn't fucking matter what he wants. So, why are you here, Corey? Is this the part where you threaten to nuke my house or some shit? Tell me to surrender for the good of everyone I care about?"

"I'm not here to make idle threats." Corey kept a smile on his face.

James didn't like it. The Shepherd reminded him of a fake-ass politician. He wanted to punch the fucker in the face.

"Then why are you here?" the bounty hunter asked.

"To have a frank and honest exchange of ideas in a less tense environment than you had with our last representative," Corey replied, leaning back in his chair. "I can understand how getting ambushed on the highway would have upset you and made you ill-inclined to take the offer."

"Does the government know you're here?" James asked. "I mean the American government, not your Council of Federated Aliens or whatever."

Corey shrugged. "I honestly have no idea. Unfortunately, access to magic means that your government has ways of tracking me that I can't easily counter. I presume they do, but it doesn't matter. We've agreed to not try to abduct or kill you. Talking to you isn't a hostile act in and of itself."

James grunted. "Whatever. So fucking talk about whatever it is you want to talk about."

Corey pointed at the bounty hunter's chest. "How much do you really understand about the purpose of that thing? *Your* intended purpose?"

"I know about all the Forerunner shit, but I'm not summoning the Vanguard, so fuck off."

The plastic smile on the alien's human guise grew wider. "Oh? And what happens after the Vanguard arrives? Do you know?"

James' mouth twitched. He hadn't thought about it much, or the implications, but when Whispy had revealed his conflicting primary directives, there was one brief detail that was chilling in its implications.

"From the look on your face," Corey stated, "you *do* know."

"Symbiont matrix-sharing," James muttered. "And the Destroyers."

*Kill the enemy,* Whispy all but shouted in his mind. *Kill the enemy. Kill the enemy. Kill the enemy.*

*Shut the fuck up, or I'll hand you over to this asshole so he can dissect you.*

*Entering partial quiescence. Full tactical abilities no longer available.*

James resisted his impulse to snort. His symbiont was pouting and flouncing, but at least he had shut up.

"Yes." Corey nodded slowly, new respect in his eyes for

James. "And do you understand the full implications of what you just said, particularly the matrix-sharing?"

"There's some way for my symbiont to transfer a lot of the defense shit to another Vax?"

Corey's expression turned grave. "Partially, at least. Interestingly enough, most Forerunners still seem to start from near scratch, from what we've seen, and to the best of our knowledge, most Vax don't leave their target planets, which might explain why your people were forced to do that. That's not always the case, though."

"I want to make one thing clear. I might have been born there, but they aren't my people." James furrowed his brow. "I wasn't supposed to be here. My parents were rebels or heretics or whatever the fuck you want to call them. They reprogrammed the symbiont and sent me to Oriceran as a young kid, but someone on Oriceran kicked me over here, and the symbiont changed me to be more human to blend in."

"As interesting and unusual as all that is, it doesn't change the fundamental truth that should the Vax come here, they could easily gain access to decades of unusual defensive adaptation by your symbiont. Something like that would be unprecedented. Do you understand that, Mr. Brownstone?" Corey raised an eyebrow in question. "And the fact that there are two directly connected worlds means a greater risk for both. Given the rarity of magic in the galaxy, they might just take you back to your home-world anyway."

James shook his head. "The way I see it, if you assholes can show up and threaten people, then so can they, and if they come, then me and Whispy need to be around to kick their asses."

"You think you have a chance against your own people?" Corey snorted. "Think about it for a second. I'm sure their symbionts will be even better adapted for battle because they didn't get prematurely sent off to another planet. We don't fully understand the Vax training process, but I will note that no Vax symbiont who has ever attacked an Alliance planet or any planet in an Alliance-adjacent system has ever been bonded to a child."

"So your big plan is that I should give you my symbiont?" James' threats to the symbiont aside, there was no way he would ever do that. He ripped open his shirt to reveal the sunken amulet and his tendril-riddled chest. "This is what you want?"

Corey shuddered in revulsion. "Yes. If you claim to care so much about Earth, the best way to protect the planet would be giving us the symbiont, even if you don't choose to come along with us. At a minimum, it reduces the sharing risk, and there's a good chance that because of your unusual background, we might be able to get viable information from it."

"Let's get one thing straight, asshole. There's no fucking way I'm leaving Earth, and considering how nuts your friend went, I'm not convinced the Nine Systems Alliance is that much better than the Vax. I need to keep Wh…my symbiont in case I need to fight you."

The other man stared at him in tense silence for several seconds. "The Alliance doesn't lay waste to planets or cut down civilians to sate murderous bloodlust. We didn't bring the war to the Vax; they brought it to us, and to other civilizations throughout the galaxy. Earth had the potential to be safe because of its unique relationship with Oriceran and the presence of magic, but let me stress the past tense: it *had*. Now that you've run around developing defenses to everything, you could easily be the key to the destruction and betrayal of your adopted planet, Mr. Brownstone."

"You don't know shit about me. Stop pretending like you do."

Corey's smile turned venomous. "You mentioned church earlier. I've studied much of human culture. It's necessary as a Shepherd, and it's taught me interesting things."

"Like what?"

"Like maybe the Vax will even give you thirty pieces of silver for your help."

James slammed his fist on the table so hard it cracked. "Fuck you, asshole," he growled.

*Quiescence terminated. Sufficient power for advanced transformation. Initiate transformation?*

*No. You will fucking do no such thing.*

*Kill the enemy. Kill the enemy. Kill the enemy.*

James couldn't say he wasn't tempted. He took a few deep breaths. If he changed now, the Shepherd would probably call in some sort of orbital strike, thinking he was going to die anyway. The one thing James had learned about these Alliance aliens was that they were all sanctimonious, self-righteous pricks.

"It seems I've agitated you, Mr. Brownstone." Corey tapped his bracelet. "But I didn't do it without purpose. I did it to make it clear that you will doom this planet if you continue as you have. If you claim affinity and loyalty to

Earth, then you'll need to at the least turn over the symbiont."

"Get the fuck out of my house before I show you how vicious a Vax can be."

Corey stood and nodded. "If you want to speak to me, just get hold of Senator Johnston. He has the means to contact me."

"I'm not fucking talking to you ever again unless it's to tear out your heart."

"I see." Corey headed toward the door. "Just keep this in mind, Mr. Brownstone. Do you honestly think the Vax will never come here?"

James shook his head, his heart still thundering and Whispy shouting for death in his mind. "I'll handle my own messes if they become a problem, but so far, the only aliens I know about who have threatened the Earth are the Alliance."

"Unfortunate." Corey opened the door and sighed. "I'm sorry we couldn't come to an understanding."

"Let me make this crystal-fucking-clear. If you come after me or any of my friends, I will track you down and I will kill you, even if I have to come all the way to your planet to do it."

They locked eyes for a few seconds before Corey turned away.

"I don't doubt you for one second, Mr. Brownstone." The alien stepped outside and closed the door.

James stared at the door as Whispy continuing ranting.

*Engage and kill enemy for maximum adaptation. Engage and kill significant tactical threat.*

*Oh, so now you're trying to goad me into it for other reasons? You can fuck off as much as he can.*

James slowly stood. With neither Shay nor Alison there, the only living thing around who could calm him would be Thomas. He'd put the dog in the backyard in case a fight broke out.

"Fucking Alliance. Fucking Vax. I hope you assholes kill each other."

CHAPTER FIVE

T he days passed without alien visitors, ambushes, or even a decent bounty daring to show his face, all of which allowed James to sink back into the pleasing mundane of his beautiful girlfriend, his dog, and his barbeque. Every once in a while, though, a stray thought about the encounter with the new Shepherd returned.

*This shit's not gonna go away, is it? The fucker's not gonna go all vigilante and start attacking AET, but I don't think he's just gonna accept my Vax ass sitting around here doing whatever the fuck I want. He doesn't seem the type. Which means I'm gonna have to solve this problem my own way.*

*Shit. Why couldn't I get the alien version of the lazy government worker who doesn't give a shit?*

As James sat in his recliner watching *Barbeque Wars: The Next Generation*, he thought through some of the implications of taking the fight to the Alliance even though he didn't think they would try anything anytime soon.

That didn't matter. A man could never be free when

another man was pointing a gun at his back and threatening to shoot.

*Fuck. I could take them out here on Earth, but they'll just send someone else, or a whole army or some shit, and it's not like I can take out a whole alien military. Not unless they land, anyway, and I doubt I'll get that lucky.*

For a brief second, a flicker of excitement popped up at the idea of challenging an Alliance army by himself. James grunted and shook his head. Whispy might constantly prod him to fight, but it wasn't like he didn't enjoy a good solid ass-kicking even when he wasn't bonded to the symbiont.

*Is that because I'm a Vax or because I'm from a shitty part of LA?*

James spared a quick glance at Shay. She had told him not to worry about the Alliance. She'd suggested they would just finish off the new Alliance asshole if he tried something, but he knew she'd been worried when they'd been confronted on the highway.

The one thing James didn't like was the idea of Shay getting caught up in an alien showdown. The last Shepherd had handed Trey and the AET their asses. As tough as Shay was, she wouldn't win against hyper-advanced technology, and she wasn't a living WMD like James and Whispy together.

*If the Alliance hurts Shay, I'll make the Vax seem like kittens in comparison. I'll fucking blow every planet they have to pieces. I hope those fuckers understand that.*

James took a deep breath and forced his attention back to the television. He wanted to push the dark thoughts out.

Everyone he cared about was safe, and he had powerful backing in the government. Shay's little experiments had even given him a new useful advantage. He didn't have anything to fear from the Alliance, who were not only afraid of *him* but also of starting a war with Earth and Oriceran.

*Everything's fine. Don't need to make shit more complicated by looking for more problems than I already have.*

"In honor of the coming Thanksgiving," explained one of the contestants on the show, a middle-aged man who insisted on wearing a suit while cooking as part of his schtick, "I've got this cranberry-centered sauce I'm going to use on the chicken for the challenge. I call it Thank Sauce, and I'm thankful for my Grandmama, who gave me the recipe."

The judges all laughed. James was unimpressed by the joke. The shit was weak as a Harriken, but the comment did remind him of something important.

"Thanksgiving, huh?" James murmured. "Damn."

Shay looked over from the table, where she was tapping away on a laptop. "What about it? Is there some special two-for-one on bounties if you bring them in on Thanksgiving this year?"

James muted the TV and looked her way. "It was a big deal at the orphanage when I was growing up. We all appreciated that it might be shitty to be in an orphanage, but at least we were taken care of, especially when the gates to Oriceran started opening and everything went to shit for a while. Thanksgiving and Christmas were the two times of the year the staff and the priests did their best to make us not feel like orphans. It used to mean something, but after I left, I stopped giving a shit. No family to share it with."

"My family was sporadic with Thanksgiving, and I never cared much either after I left home." Shay shrugged. "I was thankful every day I didn't end up dead. The turkey we had last year was tasty, though. You've got a way with meat, James. I'll give you that."

"The School of Necessary Magic doesn't send the kids home for Thanksgiving." James grunted. "That's bullshit."

"I know. It's not like I wasn't around for Alison's first two years of school." Shay chuckled. "They don't have young kids there, and it's a good way for the kids to get used to life without their families. I also assume they don't want people traveling back and forth too much from the school. They are still trying to keep it mostly secret."

"Fucking stupid, if you ask me. The gates are opening, so hiding magic seems like a waste of time. When we've got crazy-ass witches walking the streets summoning demons, hiding schools seems pointless."

Shay shook her head. "I don't know about that. To me, that seems to be all the more reason to hide that shit. There are more than a few anti-magic and anti-Oriceran terrorists out there. Would you be comfortable if the HDL or New Veil knew about that school?"

James grunted. "Just saying it might be nice if Alison could have come home so we could establish more family traditions. We do stuff at Christmas and the Fourth of July, but Thanksgiving is supposed to be the ultimate family holiday, and we even have Thomas now."

Shay eyed the dog slumbering in the middle of the

living room. "You do realize he's just a dog and not the reincarnation of that priest, right?"

"Of course I do. Just saying, family pet and shit."

"And we do have family traditions. They are just alternative traditions, such as summer bounty hunting and family ass-kicking of the guys at the agency." Shay snickered. "Those are far more interesting traditions anyway, and we can continue that shit as long as the damned aliens stay out of your way." She eyed him. "I know you've been worrying more about your little Alliance visitor than you've been willing to admit."

"I sometimes worry about the Alliance," James admitted, "but I also figure that if they had the balls to make another move right away, they probably would have done it by now. If they try anything, they'll regret it. They know that, so it's just gonna be a bunch of us snarling at one another."

"I'm with Tyler. Betting against you, no matter what the challenge, is a good way to get humiliated. You've already beaten aliens, three-headed dragons, necromancers, and zombie hordes. What's one more alien?"

"Yeah. When you say it like that, it makes sense." James nodded at the laptop. "Are you working on shit for your classes?"

Shay shook her head and turned the laptop to show him the screen. James narrowed his eyes, but from what he could tell, it was a picture of a woman skydiving in her wedding dress with a huge smile on her face.

*What the fuck? I don't care if I can survive with Whispy, I'm not jumping out of a fucking plane for our wedding. The last thing I want to do is fly on my wedding day.*

James waited for Shay to explain. It might not be as bad as he thought. For example, she could be the only one jumping out of the plane.

"Just exploring different wedding possibilities," Shay explained. "Including more…active options. I've narrowed down a lot of the unimportant crap like the non-barbeque food, bridesmaid's dresses, and basic nonsense, but I still don't have a general idea about the venue or how I'm going to make it epic but not fucking annoy all our guests at the same time. I don't want to go crazy with magic, either, because who knows how that might go wrong? At least, that's my current thought. I could be persuaded otherwise."

"No. You've got good instincts. Making shit too complicated leads to…" James blinked. "Wait. Guests?"

Shay laughed. "Most people have at least a couple of people at their weddings. Did you really think I'd have to spend all this time planning if it was just going to be a couple of witnesses in front of a judge? I'm planning the wedding, not the honeymoon."

James offered his finest, most nuanced grunt in response.

Now that Shay mentioned guests, it made perfect sense, but James had been fixated for so long on first the proposal and then Shay being responsible for the rest that he had let the reality that weddings tended to involve guests slip out of his mind. His image of the affair had previously involved a pile of Jessie Rae's with Father McCartney, Shay, and Alison.

*Shit. I was thinking about that barbeque just because I wanted some barbeque, and Mike was even asking me about guests and shit. It was so fucking obvious. Of course, the wedding's gonna be huge.*

Shay nodded. "The way I see it, we'll need to invite everyone from the agency, several of the people from my department, Peyton and his girlfriend, Heather, my girls and whatever wastes of meat they are currently dating, and Lily and most of her friends. Maria's my Maid of Honor, so that means Tyler's got to come. Is that okay?"

"I don't give a shit. Tyler's smart enough to behave at my wedding."

"I agree." Shay sneered. "I'm not inviting my parents. Shit, I don't even know if they're still alive. Pieces of crap. Surprised they haven't come sniffing around. They were always good at finding someone to leech off."

"I want to invite the people from my church," James explained. "Not just Father McCartney. The people at the orphanage. I'll let Father McCartney figure out if the kids should come. It might be boring for them."

"Okay. Have anyone else in mind?"

"Some people from the pitmaster community asked for an invitation once they heard I was engaged." James rubbed his chin. "Also Mack, Weber, and some other people from the LAPD and the Vegas PD. And the Professor. Mike and Michael and their families, of course."

Shay shrugged. "That'll be easy since Jessie Rae's will already be catering the barbeque portion of the food."

James grunted. "Senator Johnston. He said he wanted to come."

Shay laughed.

"What's so funny? You don't think we should invite him? I figure it's an easy way not to piss him off. I don't know about all this political shit, but he did basically threaten to start a nuclear war with aliens to have my back. I've got to give him a little respect for that."

"No, I don't have a problem inviting him." Shay smiled. "It's just that this is turning into a pretty big list of people, and that's really funny when you think about it."

"Why?"

"I was thinking that it wouldn't, because both of us spent most of our lives staying away from people. Neither of us went to college or worked the kind of jobs where we might have made work friends until recently, but in the end, we're going to need a big venue."

James shrugged. "Not like money's a problem. We can rent an island if we need it."

"You're right about that." Shay turned the laptop back toward her. "This is going to sound lame as shit, but I'm excited, and I've never given a fuck about weddings my entire life. Curse you, James Brownstone, for making me care about this kind of thing." She snorted. "I'm getting fucking soft."

James grinned. "Yeah, I'm kind of excited myself, especially since I don't have to do all the hard work."

"Keep it up, and I'll make you responsible for the seating charts."

*Normal life, huh? Normal marriage. Kind of? Fuck the Alliance. If they want me, they can come and get me, and I'll kick their asses all the way back to their home planets.*

James chuckled. "Maybe I should invite Sentry 8224 and tell him his wedding present will determine whether I summon the Vanguard to Earth."

Shay burst out laughing. "That would be too perfect."

Professor Smite-Williams gulped down some hearty beer as his gaze passed over a man sitting in the corner. That particular customer had been nursing a drink for an hour, and otherwise playing with his phone. The button-up shirt and khakis made the fit young man look like a businessman waiting for a date, but his calm and detached demeanor suggested he wasn't waiting for anyone.

Calm wasn't the same as carefree. Every few minutes, the man's gaze swept the room carefully and methodically. The Professor had only detected the pattern because he'd already been suspicious.

*Who are you, lad, and what are you doing here?*

When the customer had entered the Leanan Sidhe, he had been almost too relaxed and focused. Nothing about him felt right for a typical customer at the Irish pub. His movements were practiced and too obvious if one knew what to look for, as was his obvious choice of sitting in a booth with a full view of the main pub floor but with no windows at his back. The man's paranoia reminded the Professor of Miz Carson when they had first met.

*Now, who might you be, lad? It's been a long time since anyone's come sniffing around here. Are you here for James? That doesn't make sense. He doesn't drink here all that often anymore. He spends all of his time with his lovely bride-to-be, which brings us back to my question of who you are and why you've decided to visit my nice little place.*

*Time for a little test.*

When a waitress came over to give him a new beer, the Professor smiled up at her. "The nice handsome lad in the corner of the room." He nodded toward the suspicious customer. "Give him my favorite Irish Stout and tell him I'd love to talk to him if he has time."

The waitress smiled. "Of course, Professor." She set his new glass down and headed back to the bar. It was a small matter of getting the drink before heading toward the suspicious man.

Before the waitress arrived, the man stood and hurried toward the door, managing a few furtive glances at the Professor as he did.

"Well now, lad, that wasn't telling at all, was it?" the Professor muttered. "You might as well have been wearing a sign saying, 'I'm up to no good.'" He shook his head in disgust. He wasn't all that great at hiding and *he* could have done a better job, but that didn't reveal why the man had been there.

The Professor's phone chimed to let him know he had a text, and he pulled it out of his pocket. With a tap, the Professor started reading the message. His mouth turned down in a frown.

*Oh, well, this is interesting. It might explain why I had a visitor, but I'm going to need a little help.*

## CHAPTER SIX

P eyton hummed under his breath as he tapped on his keyboard. Even if Shay wasn't taking jobs nearly as often since starting full-time at the university, it didn't hurt for him to keep an eye on all the tomb raider-related forums on the dark web. If she didn't want the job, they could offer it to Lily and he could provide her support, but even the Gray Elf had cut back.

*Come on. More money for everyone, right?*

It turned out that living homeless in the tunnels had made the girl largely uninterested in the constant accumulation of huge piles of money, especially after a string of highly successful raids. She'd dropped to a raid every other month and now spent as much time helping Harry and his friends with his info broker business as raiding.

"No one's greedy anymore," the hacker mumbled. "I don't know if that's a good thing or a bad one. I thought they were both into tomb raids for the challenge as much as the money. I also don't know what it's like to be broke and living in tunnels and having to steal food, so maybe I'm too bougie to understand." He groaned. "And now I'm talking to myself. Sign of genius or insanity?"

He looked around for his cat, but the animal wasn't there to offer his evaluation.

Shay's shift from tomb raider to professor had started Peyton thinking about his future as well. With the threat of his brother long since handled, a staged comeback from his faked death wasn't out of the question. As convenient as living off the radar had been in some ways, he yearned to not worry so much about looking over his shoulder. If a former professional killer could get married and get a regular job, there was no reason why he couldn't. It'd help his relationship be less awkward, too.

*I wonder what Amber would say if she knew the truth about my past? She's a smart woman. She might already know I've got a few more secrets than I've let on. She's helping work on tech to contact aliens, among other things.*

*Would she really freak about something like me being a fake dead man? I look great for a dead guy. She'd probably be impressed that I pulled it off, even if I had Shay's help. It's hard to not exist in this day and age.*

Peyton chuckled. No one amused him more than he did. He didn't care what Shay said—he was hilarious. Not LA-comedy-club hilarious, but still damned funny, and anyone with proper taste understood that.

*What would I do if I came out of hiding? I could keep helping Lily and Shay when they needed me, but maybe some sort of business? I'd be great at cybersecurity. Working for Shay has pushed me to skill levels I never thought I'd reach. I could have corporate assholes handing me millions to defend them against whatever weak-ass script kiddie or foreign hacker is trying to break into their system.*

*That would be a nice, respectable business, and it wouldn't worry Amber if she found out about it. Hmmm. Maybe I could somehow help her with the computer end of her research. It's not like I don't have all sorts of practical experience working on unusual datasets, and I'm damned smart, if I do say so myself.*

*Handsome, smart, and King of Pizza. I'm a great catch. Not that Amber isn't a great catch, too.*

An alarm window popped up on one of his screens, and Peyton's heart rate kicked up. Had he let himself get too complacent?

"What now?" He groaned. "It better not be some parkour asshole on top the warehouse again. Is there an equivalent for scarecrows we could put up? Holographic scareteens?"

Peyton clicked his mouse and entered a few commands. When additional notes appeared, he let out a sigh of relief and chuckled.

**Intrusion Alert into System Silver #2932.**

"Oh, just one of the honeypots." Peyton rolled his eyes. "Probably just some college kid who thinks he's the shit and found the mother lode. Well, sorry, Derek or Lance or whatever your name is, you're in Peytonland now. Fake Peytonland, anyway." He clucked his tongue. "Let's see what you've got going. What did I put in 2932 again? I haven't messed with that one in a long time. I know I reorganized some of those files a few months back."

He had set up dozens of honeypot servers during his time with Shay, each populated with interesting enough if fake files, with just enough information to mislead intruders and allow him a potential way to verify an intruder's identity. They were all thoroughly isolated from the main server city and purposely had weaker defenses. Sometimes the best way to know who to look out for was to let them in the front door.

A few clicks brought up the contents of Silver #2932.

"Okay, this is a little less funny." Peyton narrowed his eyes.

The server hosted various fake alien files he'd spent weeks generating when he had been bored the previous summer. The files presented a thorough if completely fictional and fanciful account of how the US government was suppressing tentacled aliens based out of Cydonia on Mars with the help of the fictional government projects Carter and Burroughs.

Peyton was proud of the level of detail he'd put into the fake files. In a time before Oriceran they might have made a nice science fiction conspiracy story, but gates opening to a world of magic killed a lot of appetite for tales of hidden aliens. Everyone now assumed that anything alien was just a long-lost Oriceran.

Shay had been right when she and Peyton had first discovered the truth. Humanity always wanted the easy paradigm to guide their thoughts, so they'd let the truth about Oriceran provide them with that framework.

Elves were real, space aliens were not. Simple as that. Except it wasn't.

*The timing's bothering me. That Nine System Alliance guy pops over to Brownstone's place the other day, and now someone's probing around systems I control looking for alien stuff? If there's one thing working for Shay has taught me, it's that there's no such thing as a coincidence. If there's smoke, get a bunch of wizards to drown the whole area with a water spell.*

Peyton's eyes widened as he looked over the log. The intruder wasn't just looking around for alien files but was explicitly searching for files related to Aletheia, Project Ragnarök, and Project Nephilim. This wasn't some random college kid, but someone who might have a good idea of Shay's knowledge of alien activities, which pointed strongly to the government.

*Damn it! I'm not surprised, but I'm still annoyed. This is what I get for complaining the other day about how bored I was.*

Peyton gritted his teeth as he initiated a trace. This little encounter had gone from being an amusing diversion to a potential prelude to attack. The intruder's active search suggested they didn't expect they would have time to just mass-copy the files and search later, which in turn indicated they already had a good estimate of Peyton's skill level. An enemy who knew enough to show him respect was probably good enough to be annoying.

"Oh, no, you don't, you assholes." Peyton took a deep breath. "You don't realize you've stumbled into a fake server, which means it's still my advantage. You're in my kingdom now, et cetera, et cetera."

He'd need to think of cool taunts later. It wasn't important that they couldn't hear him. It was important that he amused himself.

"Time for me to deliver some counter-pain, but first, let's figure out who you are."

Peyton sighed, disappointed that no one was there to witness his glorious virtual counter-attack. Even his cat was away from the office, sleeping somewhere in the shadowy corners of Warehouse Two, needy in a way only a cat could be.

"I really need a few people sitting around me so I can stop talking to myself. Or at least so we can engage in banter. Okay, let's do this crap."

The hacker took deep breaths as his trace continued through various proxy servers. Whoever he was dealing with was damned good, and it was taking all his skill to not end up at a dead-end.

*Surprised they stumbled into the honeypot. Everything else I'm seeing suggests they're better than that.*

"Almost there. Almost there… I've got you, you sonofabitch. Ha! Boo-yah."

Peyton groaned. It was a Department of Defense server.

The intrusion abruptly ended.

Peyton sighed and leaned back in his chair, his hands on his head. "Didn't like me knocking on your door, so you ran?" He shook his head. "Time to call the boss."

Shay leaned against the wall of the office, her arms crossed, displeasure on her face. "Why would the DoD be sniffing around me? That doesn't make a lot of sense, considering the long list of people I've pissed off. If anything, the DoD seems to like James and me, especially because of the Council shit."

"I don't think it's the DoD," Peyton replied. "I think it's whoever used to pay Durand's paychecks using DoD computers as a shield, even if it's not a true proxy." Peyton shrugged. "But they still wanted to get in fast and grab specific crap from me. They knew exactly what to look for. If this had been an intrusion into something other than one of my honeypots, they probably could have grabbed the good stuff and run in the time it took me to trace the hack back to them."

"You're saying they were that good?"

"The way they detected my counter-hack and ran in an instant proves they were. I hate to say it, but I think we got lucky this time that they happened to hit the wrong server. Between their skill level and what they were looking for, there is no way these were internet randos like Derek and Lance."

"Who?"

Peyton chuckled and scratched his head. "Never mind. Long story."

Shay pushed off the wall. "Okay, so the government alien guys are looking for me. That's not news. The thing is, they were looking for Aletheia, not Shay Carson, so it turns out a little paranoia has gone a long way toward keeping me from getting killed. But it's still annoying how close they're getting." She eyed him. "A little paranoia is still good for you, too."

"I'm just the support staff," Peyton grumbled. "Why should I get killed by evil goons trying to suppress the truth?"

"Whatever happened to the King of the Internet, who was almost single-handedly responsible for getting all that useful secret-project information? I'm remembering many rants on the subject." Shay smirked. "Now you're just the hired help who has nothing to do with anything?"

Peyton saluted Shay. "The king is dead. Long live the

queen! You get out there and take those bullets for us peasants, Your Majesty."

"Very funny."

"More seriously, do you think this has to do with Alliance Corey showing up?"

Shay laughed. "Is that what we're calling him now? He sounds like a member of some boy band."

Peyton smirked. "They're ahead of us in technology. Why not boy bands?"

"Can we focus, please?"

"It's easy to remember." Peyton shrugged. "You couldn't even pronounce his real name, and from what you said James said, he wasn't sure if any human could. It'd get confusing if you just called him the 'alien' or 'the Shepherd,' since we've had a lot of those running around."

Shay groaned. "Fine, 'Alliance Corey' it is, and yes, I think it has to do with him showing up, but I don't think he's the one trying it."

Peyton nodded. "Now that you say that, I will note that the hacking techniques Erin North used were different. I don't know if that proves anything, but it's something."

"I stopped believing in coincidences when I started recognizing the symbols on James' amulet." Shay gestured toward the computer. "Maybe Alliance Corey making a move has got the government alien guys nervous, and they want to patch all the known holes out there. Aletheia is a big one."

"What about Johnston? I mean, he's played a lot of crap close to the chest, but I have a hard time believing he's clueless about stuff like them paying Durand. Even if he's not giving these guys orders, he has to have some idea what's been going on."

Shay nodded. "Probably, but it's the fucking *government*. It's a snake eating its own tail inside nested Russian dolls hidden in interlocking labyrinths. I wouldn't be surprised if half the time all these secret government guys are busy stealing from and shooting one another. They might not even know who they're screwing with."

Peyton entered a few quick commands and turned back toward her. "So you don't think this has to do with you killing Durand, then? I was also wondering if they were looking for a little payback."

Shay shook her head. "That was too long ago. If they were going to make a move, it would have happened already. These people aren't that patient, and it's not like they gave a shit about Durand. He was just a contractor to them. The fact that he got taken out just means he wasn't good enough."

"Maybe we should keep a low profile. You know, go underground or in-warehouse for a while." Peyton puffed out his cheeks for a few seconds before releasing the air. "It couldn't hurt. We both know a thing or two about hiding. Not my favorite plan, but, you know, it's a plan?" He shrugged.

Shay snorted. "The hell with that. I finally scored myself a permanent position, and if I disappear now, I'll lose any chance after all my hard work. I'm not letting a little thing like a potential death threat get in the way of tenure. It's easier to come back from the dead than get tenure these days."

"Not saying it's a great solution, and maybe it's hypocritical from an allegedly dead guy who lives in a beach-front apartment and goes walking around town all the time, but if they're sniffing around, this could end up being bad news."

"Fuck them. They don't know shit. They only know Aletheia. If they even had a clear image of me for matching algorithms, they would have already found me and tried to take me out." Shay pulled out her phone and tapped on the screen, then held it up.

It was a nice picture of her smiling for the staff directory in her department.

Peyton raised his eyebrows, slightly disturbed by the pleasant-looking Shay. "So much for keeping a low profile."

"Exactly. And what do I have to hide? The most important people in my life, including my Maid of Honor, who is an ex-LAPD AET lieutenant, know about my past, and about me being a tomb raider." Shay nodded at the computer. "But these government assholes? Screw them. They're trying to hide the existence of aliens. They've got a lot more to lose than I do if this gets messy and public, and that's not counting if they end up pissing off James."

"I know, and that's what I'm worried about."

"What do you mean?"

Peyton swallowed. "Remember when I told you about that alleged map database glitch I found a while back, concerning a surprisingly underreported major accident that pretty much wiped out an entire small town?"

"Yeah," Shay replied. "You thought it was some sort of coverup and that the government bombed a town to hide something, but then did everything they could to keep attention away from it. It's possible, but what's that have to do with anything?"

Peyton nodded. "I don't have proof, but I was able to connect it at least a little to some of this alien hunting. It might be they destroyed a town to hide the truth of aliens."

"They're ruthless assholes, but that's hardly news. What's your point?"

Peyton stared at Shay and sighed. No matter how much she'd softened with all the talk of marriage and her new job, her ruthless steel core remained. It was as impressive as it was frightening. He could barely think about the idea of rogue US government factions killing American citizens to cover up a secret without shaking a little, but it was nothing more than another Wednesday for Shay.

*I could have said they were hiding the Dread Lord Cthulhu in there and she probably would have just said, "Oh, let's go get James and kick his fucking tentacle-face back into the ocean."*

"I'm just saying," the hacker began slowly, waving his hands in front of him, "that the kind of people who'll destroy an entire town and kill hundreds of people to hide a secret won't have a problem killing a much smaller number." He pointed to himself and then her. "Like you and me, for instance. That's just two people. Team Aletheia isn't exactly an army, even if you count Lily and Osiris."

Shay snorted. "They better get me with their first bomb if they want to have any sort of fucking chance." She held up her hand with her jade ring. "Because my man got me something both pretty and practical." She headed toward the door. "At least this gives you something to do, but don't freak out. Just keep an eye on things. I'll let James know, and we'll play it by ear."

## CHAPTER SEVEN

James' phone chimed as he was about to sit in his recliner, and he grunted and pulled it out of his pocket. Unfortunate timing was forever destined to be his enemy; the one enemy he couldn't defeat with the gratuitous application of bullets, knives, or Forerunner blades.

Thomas poked his head up and cocked it, but set it down again once he realized it was a text and not something more interesting.

"Couldn't have beeped one second earlier?" James muttered. "This better not be my fucking phone company trying to make me sign up for a new plan. I thought I made that shit clear to them last time. Assholes don't have anything better to do than bother me at home."

**NEW LA COUNTY BOUNTY ALERT: (LEVEL FOUR)**
****

James grunted in pleased surprise. Things had been a little quiet, so this would be a nice change of pace.

*Huh. I set those alerts up, but I never expected to get a hit so soon after the last one. Someone's a brave fucker to come poking his nose in Los Angeles when I'm not on vacation. Maybe the idiot doesn't know I'm in town. Let's see what we've got.*

James opened the message app to check out the details for the new bounty. The level-four bounty belonged to one Gavin Vanders, a wizard who apparently liked using his powerful magic for bizarrely low-scale robberies of restaurants and bars. The small amounts stolen didn't match up with his abilities or the brutal murders accompanying many of the robberies. In his last robbery, he'd executed a waitress and a cook even though no one had tried to resist or call the cops.

*Some fucker who gets off on hurting people. I think I should teach him a thing or two about what it means to hurt someone.*

James continued reading the bounty notice. There was nothing to indicate that the bounty wouldn't be anything James couldn't handle. Vanders was a strong wizard and a specialist in a so-called "null magic," but from what James could tell, in practical terms that just meant he aimed a wand at people and burned holes through them with a shadow ray.

He'd had more than a few holes burned through him in recent years. A shadow null ray would be a nice change of pace.

*Huh. Not quite sure what that shit is, but it sounds different enough that Whispy will be happy. Almost worth going after this asshole for that alone, let alone the money or the fact this guy is such a worthless murdering shitbag. This will be almost as satisfying as that mind-control sonofabitch. Cocky murderer made a big mistake coming to my town.*

According to the bounty notice, Gavin traveled with an

entourage, which was one of the reasons the authorities suspected he was on his way to, if not already in, LA. Having too many people with him made it hard for him to travel without someone running their mouth. The new notice also meant the PDA and AET would be on the look-out. If James took too long, he might lose his chance.

"Huh," James murmured, another possibility arising in his mind. "I could use the exercise, and Whispy could use some more adaptation, but this might also be good practice for the guys. This shit seems perfect for a few guys with anti-magic deflectors and anti-magic bullets. Nothing in here about him using mind control or illusions."

He pondered the thought for a good half-minute. Training at Fort Shorty was one thing, but nothing replaced practical experience when it came to learning how to handle magical threats. The next time something like the Council arose, the men needed to be ready, and if they came at Vanders and his crew in force, they could win. James had no doubt about that.

He stared down at the phone and shook his head. It was called the Brownstone Agency, and he already let the agency handle all level three and lower bounties. If he started giving them all of the level fours, at the rate things were going in Los Angeles, he might get one decent bounty a year. That was bullshit, and it was good to lead from the front. Royce and Maria were always saying so.

Besides, even if James started Brownstone BBQ and left full-time bounty hunting, he would still want semi-regular ass-kicking action. Sometimes a man just needed to punch some bastard to relax.

*Fuck it. This guy's got a very punchable face. If it's not annoying as fuck to find the guy, I'll take him down myself. If not, I'll leave it to the guys or the cops. Just need to see if this is gonna be easy or hard, and I know one way to do that.*

James slipped his phone back in his pocket and grabbed his jacket. It was time for some old-fashioned running down a bounty, starting with a trip to the Black Sun.

Tyler offered James his standard constipated expression as the bounty hunter entered. It only made James want to bust the other man's balls harder.

*At least he hasn't tried any weird-ass tricks in a while. He might bitch about us not being friends, but he acts like we are. Don't know how I feel about that shit.*

The bar was packed, mostly with gang members, only a light smattering of higher-class criminals. A few cops nodded at him from the bar. The loud conversation didn't quiet when James entered. It wasn't like the old days. No one had any reason to fear him just stepping inside the building.

*I wasn't sure Tyler would be able to maintain the neutrality, but he's done a good job. Only a few problems since he established it. Got to give him credit for that shit. I wouldn't have thought of it. Still not sure if it's the best thing for the city or the cops, but AET are the ones maintaining it, so they must think it's a pretty good idea. Or maybe they like the idea of people being forced to respect them with other criminals around?*

James gave the cops a polite nod before making eye contact with Tyler and gesturing toward the hallway. He wasn't there for a drink, and if the other man was helpful, he'd earn far more than a nice twenty percent tip. The information broker rolled his eyes as he stepped out from behind the bar.

"This is my place, Brownstone, not yours," Tyler remarked after James walked close enough that he didn't have to raise his voice. "It's not like you get to come in here and order me around. It makes me look weak. And this isn't the White Sun. The neutrality here is maintained by the cops, not you. Keep that in mind. There's only so much of your shit I need to put up with."

"Sorry." James shrugged. "I thought you liked money. I can take my money somewhere else where people bitch less."

"I do like money," Tyler responded, uncertainty on his face.

James shrugged. "If you have the information I need, it'll be an easy and generous payday. I'm kind of in a hurry. Or you can keep bitching about how I hurt your fucking feelings, and you can go into the bathroom and cry about it until you're ready to man up and do your fucking job."

Tyler grumbled under his breath and headed down the hall toward his office, flipping off James the entire way. A few people looked their way, but most people were smart enough to mind their own damned business in a place like the Black Sun. The neutrality didn't mean they couldn't earn a target on their backs.

No criminal wanted to attract James' or the cops' attention. Neither would tag them in the building or the parking lot, but it wasn't like they couldn't track a person down later if they were given sufficient reason.

The smarter criminals kept their lackeys in line accordingly. The cops, in turn, made sure not to taunt anyone while they were there. Everyone concentrated on enjoying their drinks and bar food.

Tyler opened the door and entered his office. He waited for James to come in and close the door.

"Let me guess," Tyler began, settling behind his desk with a frown. "Since you came barging in here all of a sudden, this must be about Gavin Vanders coming to town. I doubt you give a shit about any of the other losers I've heard about lately."

James didn't bother to sit. "Yeah. I want the guy who thinks it's funny to kill waitresses. We're gonna have a little chat about fucking respect."

"So you want to know where he is?"

"Yeah." James grunted. "Don't try to feed me any shit about level fours and higher getting special respect and treatment from you. Level fours and higher rarely come to LA anymore. The only person you need to worry about pissing off is me, and we both know it. Not only that, but this guy's a real piece of shit."

Tyler snorted. "They're all pieces of shit, Brownstone. That's why they ended up with bounties."

James grunted. "Then tell me where the fucker is."

Tyler's lips curled into a sneer. "That's just it, Brownstone. I'm a businessman. I don't work for free in most circumstances."

"So?" James frowned. "I'll pay you. I always do."

"You've scared off most of the high-level trouble, and it's cutting into my profits," Tyler explained. "People don't want to pay as much money for tips about the low-level losers, and I've become accustomed to a certain lifestyle.

Fuck, it's even harder to impress Maria because she makes more money working for you than she did as a cop. Thanks for that, by the way."

"And I should care about any of this shit?"

Tyler nodded. "Yes, because it affects you. I'm going to need to make up some of those lost profits off you. I think that's fair."

"How the fuck are you going to do that?" James rumbled.

Tyler's sneer transformed into a smirk. "By charging you four times my normal fee for the information."

James grunted. "If you can give me his location today, I don't give a shit. I'll pay your fee. It's a lot of money to you. It's not a lot of money to me."

Tyler's eyes widened, the greed almost visible, and he ignored the insult. "Really? Four times?"

"Yeah. But today."

"Shit." Tyler snapped his fingers. "I should have asked for five times as much."

"Give me his location in the next five minutes, and I'll give you five times your normal fee," James replied. "Like I said, I'm in a hurry. I'm only interested in this shit if it's not too annoying, but also because this guy's a real piece of shit. I don't want him killing someone because he gets bored, so if I'm not the one tracking him down, then I need to send my guys after him right away."

Tyler laughed and pulled out his phone. "This is where being a proactive genius helps. I know exactly where he'll be for the next few hours, and it's not a restaurant. You serious about paying five times my normal fee?" He eyed James with suspicion.

"Yeah. I like it when shit's simple, and I'm willing to pay for convenience. The only witch I have in the agency is in Vegas, and I doubt Vanders has made himself easy to track anyway." James grabbed his own phone and initiated a TrollCoin transfer for the amount. "That enough?"

Tyler stared at his phone, grinning when it chimed. "Thanks for the business, Brownstone. What's the problem? Bored and desperate, so you need someone's ass to kick? Half the guys you run down are killers, and you're not normally in such a hurry."

James shrugged. "The asshole's a dirtbag, and I want to test some shit out anyway."

"'Test some shit out?'" Tyler shook his head and tapped on his phone. "I almost feel sorry for the poor bastard. *Almost.* Sending you the address now."

James didn't bother to park his F-350 in the lot, instead pulling right up to the front of the seedy dance club, The Second Circle. The stylized red-orange letters spelling out the name had been designed to mimic flames.

The thumping bass from inside the club already annoyed him. He hated having to take assholes down in places like this.

*Huh. If I end up in actual Hell, it'll probably be some shit like this, and offering me a tray of ribs I can never reach.*

Shay loved dance clubs, but if someone came out and told James they were a twisted Oriceran plot designed to fuck humans up, he wouldn't have been surprised.

*Why do people subject themselves to that shit? They really hate being able to hear?*

James opened the driver's door, jumped down, and headed toward the huge bouncer. A few other people waiting to get in backed away when they saw him, although a few others took pictures with eager smiles.

The bouncer frowned and stared at James. It was rare that a human managed to make James look small, but as far as the bounty hunter was concerned, that just made the bouncer a larger and easier-to-hit target if he needed to beat his ass. He didn't mind a man doing his job, but he didn't have time for bullshit.

James marched toward the door. The bouncer interposed himself between James and his destination, his meaty palm out.

"Whoa there, freakface," the bouncer commanded with a frown. "Do we look like the kind of place that has fucking valet parking for your piece-of-shit truck?" He snorted and pointed at the truck. "And this isn't some club for cowboys or whatever the fuck you're supposed to be with that ugly-ass duster. So why don't you yippee-kai-fucking-away across town?"

James looked down at his gray coat. It did resemble a duster, but that was a thin fashion line to hang a cowboy insult on.

*Maybe I should be wearing dusters. Need more pockets, though.*

"I'm not a fucking cowboy, asshole," James rumbled. "And respect my fucking truck. It's a classic."

"You are whatever the fuck I say you are, cowboy, and I don't give a shit about your ancient piece-of-shit truck."

James let out a low growl, but he let the insult pass. He was there for the bounty, not some random bouncer.

The bouncer looked James up and down. "Wait, do I know you? I think I've seen you somewhere before. Did I kick your ass out of here before? Don't think because you've got a few tats that I'm intimidated by your ass. I kicked some Russian Mafia guys out of here just the other night, and I've gone up against Kilomea and won."

*So have I, and a lot worse.*

James glared at the man. "There's a level-four bounty in your club right now by the name of Gavin Vanders. I'm gonna go in there, beat him down, and drag his ass out. You can help me get the people out of the club so I can go beat his ass down without anyone else getting hurt, or you can fucking piss me off to make a point while some murderous piece of shit dances inside with his fucking friends."

"I don't think…" The bouncer winced and backed up. "Oh, shit, now I recognize you. You're James Brownstone."

"Yeah." James grunted. "Surprise, asshole."

The man put his hands in front of him. "We don't need trouble, Brownstone. If you know he's in here, can't you just wait until he comes out and nail him then?"

James pointed at the door. "Here's what you're gonna do. You're gonna get everyone out of there, and because Vanders is an arrogant sonofabitch, he won't run. I don't want to wait around until his ass comes out. You're going to go in there, tell the DJ to cut the music and then tell Vanders that James Brownstone is coming for him. Do we have an understanding?"

The bouncer swallowed before offering a shallow nod and rushing inside the club.

James reached under his shirt and pulled the metal separator off his amulet. His face twitched as the all-too-familiar hot pain of Whispy sinking into his chest and burrowing tendrils through it followed.

Several people snapped pictures, but all they'd get for their efforts was a grimacing James because of his shirt. Enough people had seen the amulet to know he had a special artifact, but most still had no clue what it was or how it worked.

*Initiation,* Whispy sent.

*Time for a little training,* James responded.

## CHAPTER EIGHT

James waited with a frown as people streamed out of the club, most in a hurry but none looking scared. Some of the departing people rushed by with their cameras up to snap pictures of him as they fled. One woman flashed him.

*Seriously? There's a fucking bounty in there, and you're all acting like this is some movie premiere.*

"Kick his fucking ass, Brownstone!" shouted one man in a shirt that had more colors than should be legal. His words were slightly slurred, and he swayed as he walked.

Another man jogged by with his phone up. "Do that shit where you kick them through a wall. Fuck those bitches for thinking they could come into Brownstone Country, bro! Boo-yah, motherfuckers!"

*Don't know if I should like this shit or be annoyed by it.*

A few other men and the occasional woman offered their less-than-helpful advice and suggestions as they continued streaming out of the club. Their continued movement away from the club suggested they might be convinced of his eventual victory, but they also didn't want to be present when he delivered the pain.

*Good. That means they're not total fucking morons, so I can go all out if I need to without any trouble. No hostages or shit like that mind-control asshole. It'll be a nice, clean fucking fight.*

A couple of minutes passed before the flood of people turned into a mere trickle, and finally, the bouncer came out, sweat covering his pale face.

"Just so you know, man, I called the cops," the bouncer explained as he headed into the parking lot. "I told them you were here and what you were doing, so you can just chill and wait for them. I'm sure you'll get your money just for being here."

James shrugged. He wasn't really there for the money. It was just spice.

"They aren't going to show up anytime soon then. It'd be a waste of resources to scramble AET for a level four when I'm on scene. Everyone out? I didn't hear any fire alarms. No one took the emergency exits?"

"I told everyone to go out the front." The bouncer frowned. "I didn't want someone getting stuck behind the building in case you blow it up."

"If I damage the place, I'll pay for it." James shrugged. "And I don't blow up buildings all that often, and not for level fours."

The bouncer's face scrunched in confusion and fear. He shook his head. "Why did I take the extra shift? Sometimes life gets too fucking complicated, even by the standards of LA." He sighed and jogged into the parking lot.

"Yeah," James mumbled. "I feel that. Sorry."

*Moderate potential adaptation,* Whispy reported. *Engage and kill targets for maximum adaptation.*

*No killing,* James thought back. *The bounty on this asshole isn't dead or alive. Probably the same for his friends.*

*Engage and kill targets for maximum adaptation,* Whispy insisted, a hint of annoyance coming through the mental link.

Of all the things James had managed to teach the symbiont in the last couple of years, the value of money wasn't one of them. It made him wonder how things worked on the Vax homeworld.

*Oh, wait. I don't know if there are any bounties on his entourage. Fuck them. We'll kill them if they get in the way. If they're hanging out with an asshole who'll kill waitresses and cooks at restaurants, they're pieces of shit.*

*Kill the enemy, kill the enemy, kill the enemy.*

*Yeah, just not the one.*

James pulled out his .45 and marched into the club. The thumping beat from before had long since died and the main lights had been turned on, revealing a room in need of a good sweeping and scrubbing. There were a surprising number of shirts and shoes strewn about, along with bottles and cups.

*Everyone looked calm, but they just dropped their shit and left.*

A man in a black t-shirt and jeans that must have been purchased from the Tight-ass Jeans Company stood in the center of the dance floor with an obsidian-tipped wand in his hand. Half a dozen other men surrounded him, all holding thin glowing knives. Everyone had murder in their eyes.

Excitement radiated from Whispy.

James didn't raise his gun. "Before we get started, I just want to be sure. You Gavin Vanders? If you're not Gavin Vanders, I don't give a fuck. This is about bounty shit, and I'm not here to start anything with random assholes."

The wizard tapped his wand on his shoulder. "Yes, I am Gavin Vanders." He sighed. "I was expecting this to happen. Fuck. People warned me, but I didn't think it'd happen to me."

"What are you talking about?"

"Come on, Brownstone. Everyone says that if you're even remotely big shit, you shouldn't go to LA because the Granite Ghost will come after you." Gavin tapped his forehead with his wand. "That was what everyone told me when I said I was heading to LA, and I blew them off."

James grunted. "It's true, but only if you have a bounty. And you do, Vanders—level four, armed robbery and murder, among other things."

Gavin smiled brightly. "Yeah, I do have a bounty, but I'm still glad I came here."

"You are? Why the fuck is that?"

Gavin flourished his wand and bowed. "Big fan. I've got to say, you do look pretty fucking tough in person, Brownstone. It would have been disappointing if I came here and you looked shorter, or the voice was fake."

James narrowed his eyes. "You're a big fan of a bounty hunter? How the fuck does that make any sense?"

Gavin shrugged. "You're a tough asshole. I can get behind that. It's not like I have any special loyalty to the underworld. So, yeah, big fan."

"Huh. I was half-expecting you to give me a big speech

about how I'm nothing and you're going to beat my ass down and shit. That's what most of you assholes say."

Gavin snickered. "Nah, come on. Sure, a man can inflate his reputation a little, but not too much. Everyone saw what you did at that amusement park fight. Anyone taking you on and thinking you can't kick a lot of ass is a special kind of stupid."

James holstered his weapon, the motion causing the men with knives to raise their weapons. There was a slight shimmer around them as they did. He reached into his pocket and felt for a small magic coin Shay had given him. He might get to test Shay's jumpstart method in an actual fight.

*Kill the enemy,* Whispy insisted.

*If necessary. And the way this guy is talking, I'm guessing this gonna end with some ass-kicking.*

"If you understand I'm not to be fucked with, why don't you make this shit easy and surrender?" James gestured to the man's lackeys. "I don't even know who these fuckers are, let alone if they have bounties, so this just has to be you going in. They can walk."

Gavin sighed. "That's the thing, Brownstone—I don't think prison would agree with me. Too hard to schedule a good lay, you know what I mean? And I don't think I'd like the food."

His men all laughed.

*That shit was weak.*

"You had your chance to run, but you're still here," James rumbled. "If you know you can't win, then what you are hoping for? That I'll let you go? I don't let bounties go because they say they're fans. I don't care about what tragic fucking backstory you have, either, about how you needed to rob all those places for your sister's surgery or whatever."

Gavin shook his wand in front of his face. "No, no. It's not that I can't win. It's just that I'm not stupid enough to think you aren't tough. And tragic backstory?" He snorted. "I actually inherited a hundred million dollars when I was eighteen. I don't commit crimes because I need the money. I commit crimes because it's fun, and it beats being bored." He shrugged. "What's the point of being a rich wizard if I can't rob the occasional place because I feel like it?"

James grunted. "Aren't you just the perfect example of a pile of shit?"

*Kill the enemy*, Whispy demanded again.

*Strongly considering it.*

"Probably," Gavin responded, "but I'm a pile of shit willing to offer you twice my bounty to let me walk. You're a bounty hunter, not a cop. Come on, Brownstone, you might be rich from all your bounties, but you're still all about money. You don't have a sworn duty to take me down." He shrugged. "And, shit, if you track my ass down again, I'm willing to offer you the same deal. I've got plenty of money."

"I don't get it." James furrowed his brow. "You knew I might come, and you were still sitting here partying?"

"Sure, because I figured I'd just offer this deal." Gavin frowned. "I didn't think you would track my ass down so quickly, but that proves you got something going on upstairs, too." He tapped the tip of his wand in his palm. "So, what do you say, Brownstone? Want to make the easiest money you've ever earned, or are we going to have a pointless fight where someone might get hurt?"

James cracked his knuckles. "Last chance. Surrender, or this is gonna end with you hurt. I also can't guarantee your little bitch posse won't end up dead."

Gavin pointed his wand at James, some of his earlier easy manner sliding off his face. "Just because you're tough doesn't mean you won't get hurt, Brownstone. I've got a few tricks I don't think you've seen before."

*Engage enemy for maximum adaptation,* Whispy demanded.

James pulled his gun out again. He was surprised the bounty and his men hadn't attacked him immediately. He pointed the gun at Gavin's leg. "You got more tricks than a three-headed dragon?"

"Huh?" Gavin blinked. "What the fuck are you talking about?"

"Just saying I've seen a lot of shit." James fired.

A shield flashed around Gavin and the bullet fell to the ground, not crushed or showing any sign of impact.

*So, it doesn't deflect. At least that'll cut down on collateral damage.*

*Kill the enemy,* Whispy chanted.

James whipped his gun to the side and fired at one of the knife-wielders. The bullet also ended up on the ground. He emptied his magazine between the rest of the men and the wizard before holstering his gun.

Gavin looked pained. "That wasn't impressive. Come on, Brownstone. We both know you've got more than that. That shit right there was insulting. Fuck, this is embarrassing for both of us."

"Hey, why use the top-grade shit if you don't need it?" James shrugged.

The men all laughed.

James didn't. "This is the part where people start dying." He pulled off his coat and tossed it to the side, then removed his knife sheath and holster. No reason to lose a perfectly good holster when he activated advanced mode. "And you're not gonna die, Gavin, but I am gonna fuck you up." He reached into his pocket and pulled out the magic coin.

"We'll see about that." Gavin pointed his wand and shouted an incantation, and a ray of pure darkness shot from his wand. It shot forward, obscuring the area around it as if eating the light.

James hissed as pain blasted from his shoulder and suffused the rest of his body.

*Yesssss,* Whispy sent. *New adaptation in progress. Heavy regeneration in progress.*

James looked down at his throbbing shoulder, wondering why it hurt so badly. There was a huge hole through it.

*Huh. That explains it.*

"Damn!" Gavin shouted slapping his leg. "I didn't think it'd work so well. Fuck. You can see clean through him." He laughed. "See that shit?"

The men all laughed and pointed.

Despite the injury, James wasn't actually that angry, and the wound hurt less than many similar injuries he'd suffered before, perhaps an artifact of the magic used. Whispy's joy over the new damage source further dampened any irritation.

It was the perfect time for a test.

James slipped the coin under his shirt and against the amulet, his teeth gritted. It might not be the worst pain ever, but it was still pain. "That shit hurt, Vanders."

Gavin waved his wand. "Offer's off the table, Brownstone. I'll let you leave, but I'm not paying you a dime. The fact that you're not wetting your pants and screaming in pain proves that you live up to the hype, so I still have mad respect for you."

*Do it, Whispy.*

*Utilizing alternate power source. Advanced transformation in progress.*

The bioarmor spread from the amulet, covering the wound in his shoulder, and his blade appeared. James took a deep breath and pointed the weapon at Gavin.

"Damn, there it is." The wizard frowned. "Don't do this, Brownstone. I've still got respect for you. It might help my rep to kill you, but I really don't want to, especially after seeing you take that null ray like it happens to you every day. It'd be a fucking waste of a kick-ass man."

"Now you've got my attention," the bounty hunter rumbled. "You should have put that shit through my head, but to be honest, not sure even that would have finished me off. I don't think you understand who you're fucking fighting, asshole."

"Too bad." Gavin shook his head. "What a fucking waste." He fired another null ray.

The attack struck James square in the chest, digging through the armor but not penetrating much into his chest. The attack left a mild surface burn, but the pain was nothing compared to James' shoulder.

"What the fuck?" the wizard yelled.

Tendrils of the armor threaded to seal the new hole, and the pain in James' shoulder started to ebb.

*Regeneration still in progress,* Whispy reported. *Primary adaptation achieved. Kill the enemy.*

"My turn, fucker," James growled. He charged the wizard.

Gavin took a step back, confusion and fear in his eyes, and his men rushed forward with their glowing knives. James backhanded one man, who spun through the air and landed on his arm with a loud snap. Being unconscious kept him from screaming.

Two more men stabbed at James, but their weapons bounced off without a scratch. James gutted one man before spinning and slashing the throat of the other. Their blood coated the floor, and James made a mental note to make sure to offer the club owner extra money to hire special cleaners.

*Kill the enemy,* Whispy cheered. *Kill the enemy. Kill the enemy.*

Gavin fired off another ray, but the new attack barely penetrated the top few layers of armor. Terror seized the wizard's face as his remaining men continued slashing at James with their magic knives. James stabbed another man and smashed him against one of his friends before pulling the blade out.

The surviving member of the entourage dropped his knife and ran for the door. James didn't bother chasing him. He wasn't there for random thugs.

James stepped toward the wizard. "You know what they say, Vanders. Be careful what you fucking wish for."

Gavin raised his wand, his arm trembling. He launched a large fireball toward his tormentor and it exploded around James, but it didn't accomplish much more than stinging his eyes, even without a helmet.

"Bring it, bitch," James rumbled. "Because that shit was just fucking embarrassing for both of us."

An ice lance came next, and it shattered into thousands of pieces against his chest. The impact did jostle him, though, increasing the ache from his shoulder.

*Definitely regenerating slower.*

*Limited power available from alternate power source,* Whispy responded.

James reached down and grabbed a knife from one of the dead men.

"What the fuck are you doing, Brownstone?" Gavin shouted.

"Making this bullshit worthwhile." James placed the blade against the center of the armor.

*Alternate power usage in progress,* Whispy reported.

James tossed it to the ground and grabbed another knife and repeated the process.

*Regeneration accelerated.*

"You know why it's your lucky day, Vanders?" James asked.

"Fuck you! Die, shithead!" Gavin shouted his next incantation and a massive electrical bolt blasted into James.

*Maximum adaptation already attained,* Whispy reported. *Previous attacks indicate minimal additional adaptation potential. Kill the enemy. Find and engage stronger enemy.*

James picked up the other knives and drained them. "It's your lucky day because I decided I need to test some shit, which meant I didn't finish you off as quickly as possible. You got a little more time without some serious pain, asshole."

"I'm a fucking wizard, Brownstone, not some gangster," Gavin snarled. "You're not going to win."

The wizard spent the next thirty seconds pelting James with every element and material the man could summon, but none of his other attacks approached the damage of his initial null ray. Whispy's excitement continued to fade, and his requests for immediate termination increased.

*Whispy*, James thought, *is that enough power for extended advanced transformation?*

*Yes, but stability limited with alternate power sources used.*

*Fine, just do it.*

The silver-green metallic tendrils spread, encasing James' entire body in armor. His helmet formed, blinding him, and his claws extended. It was an odd sensation wearing the full armor without the familiar all-consuming rage. A few seconds of pain in his eyes preceded his vision returning with a wider field of view.

"You're fucking finished, Vanders," James thundered.

Gavin raised his wand again, and several of the massive speakers tore away from the roof and hurtled toward James. The bounty hunter didn't even bother to dodge as they slammed into him. The impact barely even made his shoulder hurt. Most of the previous pain had vanished.

*Kill the enemy*, Whispy demanded. *Limited power available for extended advanced mode.*

*Guess I'm not gonna end up in Forerunner mode just from draining artifacts, huh?*

*Insufficient power for Forerunner transformation. Primary power source necessary.*

James grunted. It was time to finish this shit. He charged Gavin and slammed an armored foot into the man. The wizard flew back and crashed into a nearby wall with a crunch. His head lolled forward, but he was still breathing.

"Fan request, asshole," James rumbled. "And a little payback for all the people you've hurt."

*Extended advanced mode instability,* Whispy reported. *Insufficient power to maintain form.*

*Revert. I don't need that shit anymore. This battle is over.*

The armor pulled away from his body and flowed back into the amulet. James rolled his shoulder a few times. The hole was gone, but a slight ache remained. Getting pissed was definitely more effective than draining artifacts, but it was nice to have a backup plan.

"Shit. Now I *do* need the cops here."

## CHAPTER NINE

Senator Johnston looked up from his computer screen as a frowning bald man in a black suit entered his office. It was Senior CIA Agent Timothy Franklin, and unlike the last time, he was expecting the man.

*These CIA types should mix it up, the senator thought. They should start wearing more earth tones or something. That might be interesting. As it is, I swear, every time I see one of these guys, they're wearing basically the same suit and have the same haircut. Well, maybe not Tim, but he had the same haircut back when he still had hair.*

"Thanks for coming, Tim." Senator Johnston motioned to the chair in front of his desk as the new arrival closed the door. "Take a seat. It's been too long. Been a few months since we last talked face to face, if my old memory hasn't failed me."

Tim nodded. "Unless mine failed too, that's about right. There have been a lot of things happening behind the scenes since then."

The CIA agent pulled out a small metal cube and set it on the desk before taking a seat.

Senator Johnston frowned. "This room's secure. You don't need that gadget."

Tim shook his head. "I haven't lived this long by not making sure every time. No offense, Angus. After everything I've seen in my career, let alone the last few years, I can't be sure about anything. For all I know, you could be an alien clone or an Oriceran illusion."

"And I thought *I* was paranoid. Just trying to lower your stress, but I hear you. Things are a lot more complicated, true enough." The senator chuckled. "I'm surprised you haven't stroked out yet. You've never been a laid-back man, and these last couple of decades have been tough on people like you and me."

Tim snorted. "I'm too stubborn to have a stroke. I have a lot of unfinished business. What's this all about? You said it was important. I'm assuming your granddaughter isn't selling cookies."

Senator Johnston rolled his chair forward. "I trust you're fully up-to-date on the Nine Systems Alliance situation? It's my understanding that you're in the loop on all of the most important details. I don't mind explaining, but it'll save us both a lot of time if you already know."

Tim nodded. "Trust me, I know far more about this garbage than I want to." He shook his head. "I remember when I used to worry about a single alien species, and now we're in communication with a whole group of them. Plus, we're caught up in their mess with those Vax. I feel like Earth got dragged into an intergalactic war when we were doing nothing but minding our own business. At least the

Oricerans had the decency to have their wars under control when the gates started opening."

"True enough, but I don't see how these new creatures being from outer space makes much difference when compared with the Oricerans. Advanced tech might as well be magic. After the open return of magic, it's hard for me to be flustered by anything." Senator Johnston shrugged.

"That's the problem. Oriceran's one planet, but now we've got a whole galaxy to worry about. At least with the magic, we theoretically have the Oricerans backing us up, and simple time will make magic stronger on Earth. However, some of the alien tech we've recovered is on a whole different level. Forget reverse engineering it." Tim grimaced. "It'd take us centuries to even begin to understand the most basic principles involved." He reached into his jacket pocket and pulled out a small crystalline slab only a few inches in height and width. He tossed it on the desk. "Right now, we're like birds who have gotten our hands on a phone. We can use it to crack nuts, but that doesn't mean we understand it."

Senator Johnston peered at the slab. "What's this? Alien nutcracker?" He chuckled. "I could use one."

Tim shrugged. "Hell if I know, and that's the problem. One of my guys picked this up a few years back. It's an artifact I keep on me to stall if I ever get grabbed by foreign intel. It's definitely alien, but we've never been able to figure out its function—if it even has one—or what species it comes from. For all we know, it could be nothing more than an alien bookmark. The only reason we know it's alien is because it was found in an area with an energy signature similar to some of the other alien species we've dealt with, but the design of the slab is unlike anything else we've seen from them. A mystery. That's the problem with these damned aliens: too many mysteries."

Senator Johnston gazed at the slab for a long moment before looking back up at the CIA agent. "I don't understand. How does this help you if you get grabbed if you don't even know what it does?"

"If I'm grabbed, I'll just lie about it being a data storage device." Tim tapped the slab. "This is a perfect illustration of what I'm talking about. The best minds on this planet, men and women who have researched alien technology for years, have examined this object. I've had some friendly magicals do it as well, and you know what they've been able to tell me about it? You know what the sum total of all that careful exploration and research is?"

"What?"

"It's made of a crystalline material not found on Earth, and it has patterns inside." Tim scoffed. "That's it. That's the best that Earth knowledge and magic can discern. I'm not some idiot with a conspiracy website on Mars. I'm a senior CIA official with access to magical and technological specialists and billions of dollars, and I have no fucking clue what this is. It could be a toaster, or it could be alien porn."

Senator Johnston eyed the other man, letting his apprehension show on his face. "We all know we're behind in a lot of ways, which is why we need to take every advantage we have. Or are you saying it's hopeless, Tim? I have a hard time believing that, but if you do feel that way, it's fine. I don't believe that, and I refuse to continue forward under that assumption."

Tim shook his head. "If it was hopeless, I wouldn't bother getting up in the morning, but I am saying we've been damned lucky. Relying on luck is not a good strategy for defending either your country or your planet from hostile threats with power far beyond our own."

"Some of it hasn't been luck. Even if she turned out to be disagreeable, the previous Shepherd assigned to Earth was watching over us, which meant we had some protection. The Nine System Alliance is keeping at least some threats away."

"That's like saying you don't have to worry about local muggers because the local Mafia would be pissed at them." Tim picked up the crystal slab and slid it back into his pocket. "The Alliance has already threatened to use advanced weapons against Earth, and the previous Shepherd was killing people without our explicit permission. The Alliance is just as much a sword pointed at us as our enemies, and that's assuming Brownstone doesn't go bad. Again, I'd rather not rely on luck."

"This time it's not a matter of luck." Senator Johnston chuckled. "Being a politician means learning how far you can trust people, and I'm pretty damned good at it. You might be alive because you're paranoid, but I've been re-elected this many times because I know how to read people and take advantage of that."

"Does that mean we're depending on your gut to make sure we haven't made a horrible mistake in not turning over Brownstone?" Tim raised an eyebrow. "Sorry, Angus. I don't trust you enough to leave Earth's safety to your gut."

"No, this isn't about just my gut. In every negotiation, you bring leverage to the table. Sometimes negative leverage, and sometimes positive leverage." The senator leaned back in his chair and laced his fingers together. "I've already brought positive leverage by helping to protect Mr. Brownstone from the Nine Systems Alliance, and I've got plenty of backup plans for James Brownstone. He's one man. Even if he's a powerful alien, he's still just one. I'm not very worried about him threatening the Earth. One man can always be dealt with."

Tim locked eyes with the senator, disbelief on his face. "What's your big plan? Sending him to the World in Between? Considering how much anti-magic he's already displayed, that might not even work, and these Vax can open portals. He might develop that ability and somehow get out."

"Doubtful, and yes, that's one plan, but I've got others to slow him down—if and *only* if he goes bad."

"Such as?"

Senator Johnston grinned. "Bury him in ten tons of concrete, just as an example, and toss him into the Mariana Trench. That would at least slow him down, I bet."

Tim blinked. "Seriously?"

"That's one of them." Senator Johnston lowered his hands. "For now, I'm choosing to treat him as an asset until such time as he proves not to be. He's not the problem, and he's not why I asked you to come."

"Okay, so I don't want to be more of a cranky asshole than I already am, but why *am* I here, Angus?" Tim gave him a questioning look.

"I'm just doing the same thing you've always tried to do: make sure there are backup options. That's what we're here for, to discuss more of those."

"More options? Other than tossing Brownstone into the Mariana Trench? I can loan you a matter transformation gun, but I'm not sure if it'd work on him."

Senator Johnston chuckled. "This isn't about Brownstone, but about his biggest fans, the Nine Systems Alliance. I don't care if the two I've talked to from the Alliance are aliens. People are people, whether they have pointy ears or wings or were born on a planet light-years away."

"And what's that supposed to mean?"

"I can smell desperation on people, and I know it's only a matter of time before the Alliance does something stupid because of desperation. It could be tomorrow or it could be ten years from now, but it'll happen. When it does, we need to be ready to counter that."

Tim nodded gravely. "You're talking about interstellar war?"

"Maybe I'm just talking about stopping the Apocalypse."

"You could give Brownstone up."

Senator Johnston snorted. "Brownstone's just one problem. Oriceran and Earth have a unique relationship. Today, it might be Brownstone the Alliance is pissed about, but what happens when we start opening magical portals into space? The Alliance doesn't have that ability. They could decide to try to take us out before we get that far."

Tim nodded. "Not that I disagree with any of that, but how do you intend to be ready? It's not like we can wave a wand and improve our industrial and technological base by centuries. We're just starting to get going again after all the chaos that followed the gates opening."

"Exactly. We need to take advantage, not only of our

technology, which is behind, but our magic, which is the one thing the Alliance doesn't have."

"How?"

"I managed to get some help to point me in the right direction for the recovery of a little something that might be helpful if this Nine Systems Alliance turns hostile," the senator explained. "I'm confident Brownstone will help us if he's still around, but he can't do much if they decide to bomb us from orbit, and Oriceran magic has its limits once you get off the planet. Even a lot of the toys your people have collected won't be helpful in that kind of situation."

Tim snorted. "From what I've seen of this Nine Systems Alliance, they're a little behind some of the aliens my people have dealt with."

"Maybe in absolute technology, but those other aliens barely cared about the Earth, and they weren't planning anything other than observation. They weren't wetting their pants about a Vax on Earth or magic, either." The senator took a deep breath. "Anyway, the point is, I've got good people who can be trusted to help to recover what I need as the first step of my backup plan, but I'm worried about interference from other people who might decide they want to handle this situation in a different way. People who have far more experience dealing directly with aliens than I do.

"You're talking about Fortis." Tim narrowed his eyes. "Or what's left of them, anyway."

Senator Johnston sighed and shook his head. "Yes. It's one of the reasons I've reached out to certain people outside the government who are used to dealing with dangerous operatives to recover what we need. I'm a US senator. I'm used to depending on the other parts of the government to watch out for me. All this spy versus spy crap is annoying, especially when the people I'm worried about are from my own country." He frowned. "People have attempted to assassinate me in the past. That's fine; it's part of serving my country, but I can't have those dangerous cowboys undermining my attempts to protect the country and the planet."

"Trust me, I know how annoying that is. Fortis agents have tried to kill my people and me more than a few times." Tim reached into his pocket and pulled out a small stress ball, then gave it a tight squeeze. "It took us a while, and we pushed them back, but there's no way of being sure we got them all. You're right to worry."

Senator Johnston scowled. "I'll be honest, Tim. I don't care if you got them all or get the rest now. I only care if they don't screw up the operation I'm about to initiate. I need your help to help keep those Fortis bastards from taking what they don't need. This operation might prove critical to the future defense of Earth."

A cold look entered Tim's eyes. "And you don't care how I get it done? You *do* understand what I'm saying, right?"

"Ruthless men have to be handled through ruthless means, especially when the fate of the world is at stake."

"And you're not worried that makes us like them?"

Senator Johnston shook his head. "They signed up for the game, and they know that if they lose, they could end up dead. That's different than them killing innocent Americans who didn't do anything other than be in the wrong place at the wrong time. Brutal destruction and mindless hoarding of alien tech isn't the way to prepare the country or the planet for danger. You would have thought we had learned our lesson when we hid magic."

"Fair enough," Tim replied. "I'll get my best people to run interference for you, but I can't guarantee they'll be able to stop everything. You need to make sure whoever you're using on your end can handle themselves."

"Don't worry. Your people just need to stop enough. The people I'm going to have move on this will be able to deal with whatever else trickles through."

Tim squeezed his stress ball again, a nervous look on his face. "And who might that be?"

Senator Johnston grinned. "Shay Carson and James Brownstone."

## CHAPTER TEN

James lifted his knife, ready to dice his enemy into pieces. It was nothing personal. He just needed to chop his target into finer chunks. With a few quick movements, he reduced the large onion to smaller squares. He grabbed another onion, ready to repeat the process.

*This sauce is gonna be fucking great. I should have made it a while ago.*

Thomas sat by James' feet, looking up at James with wide, pleading eyes. He whimpered.

"You can't have onions," James rumbled. "Go eat some of your dog food. You like that shit. You eat tons of it, anyway, so go eat some more."

Thomas whined and shuffled off to his bowl, his tail drooping.

*Tough to be a dog. A lot of high-quality barbeque-related shit you can't have. It's not fair.*

James shook his head, his heart filled with pity for the poor, suffering animal denied the full breadth of the glories of human food.

*We don't dominate this planet because we make sure no one else gets above us on the food chain. We dominate this planet because we can eat almost anything.*

*Like fugu. Some guy in Japan in the past actually had to sit down and say, 'Hey, everyone keeps dying from that poison fish, but I'm sure there's a part that's not poisonous and still tastes good.'*

Pain shot through James' finger. His lack of concentration had led to his knife slicing his finger. He lifted his hand and shook it before wiping off the blood with a paper towel and taking a look. Considering how many times he'd been shot, stabbed or electrocuted, even without the amulet, a little slice of the finger was almost nothing. He could have taken the entire tip off and not been too concerned.

"Huh. Deep, but not worth wasting much time on." James grabbed some electrical tape out of a nearby drawer and taped the throbbing wound. He could put on Whispy later and regenerate.

A simple cut wouldn't get in the way of his sauce preparation. He wanted to try out this new sauce and get feedback as soon as possible so he could be ready for the spring contests.

James continued his preparation, ignoring the mild throbbing in his finger.

*This shit is gonna be some of the best I've ever made.*

Shay wandered into the kitchen a few minutes later, and she stopped and stared at his hand. James had already moved on to sautéing the diced onions in bacon grease and nodding to himself in satisfaction, the wound a distant thought in the back of his mind.

"Why do you have electrical tape on your finger?" Shay asked. "Is that some weird artifact thing I don't know about?"

"I cut my finger with the knife," James replied. "And I needed to stop the bleeding. It's deep and shit, but I'll use Whispy later and have him fix it." He nodded to his pan. "I'm doing this right now."

"And, like, putting a bandage on didn't occur to you?" Shay stared at him, disbelief on her face. "You're using electrical tape instead? Why?"

"The tape was closer, and I didn't want to fuck up my rhythm on sauce prep." James shrugged.

"Okay. Your finger—if it falls off later, don't blame me." Shay chuckled and headed to the dining room table. "So, let's talk about music. I assume you can do that while watching your blood-soaked onions."

James glanced down to make sure he hadn't leaked any blood onto his diced onions before shaking his pan slightly. "Music? What about it?"

"We need to decide on music for the wedding and reception. You barely listen to music unless you're counting the first few seconds of podcasts, so it's hard to know what will annoy you. I've collected samples of all sorts of types of music I like, instrumental and otherwise."

James furrowed his brow. "Not only do I not listen to music much, I don't really care much about music, either."

The pan sizzled.

Shay smirked. "Is that because you can't put sauce on it and eat it?"

James grunted. "I'm not saying that's the reason, but that is true."

"I'll keep that in mind." Shay sighed and scrolled on her phone with her thumb. "You don't have any strong preferences then, pro or con? Just something to narrow the choices?"

"Yeah, no strong preferences. You do what you want."

"You should never say that. It gives me ideas." Shay gave him an evil grin.

"Ideas?" James replied. "Like what?"

"Kilomea mariachi band. That would be different. Maybe even epic."

James shook his onions again before blinking and turning back toward Shay. It'd taken him a moment to parse what his fiancée had said. "*Kilomea mariachi band?*"

Shay nodded. "Those were the words that came out of my mouth, yes."

"Do they even have Kilomea mariachi bands? I don't think I've seen one ever, either in southern California or Mexico. Not saying they don't exist, but, shit…"

"I don't know." Shay looked uncertain, the evil gleam fading from her eyes. "Maybe? Stranger things have happened. I don't remember having seen any, but elf pitmasters used to not be a thing either. Shit, there are elves in heavy metal bands, so why not Kilomea in mariachi bands?"

"True enough." James furrowed his brow. "I kind of like the idea. At least it wouldn't be boring."

Shay laughed. "Okay, you called my bluff. We're not gonna have a Kilomea mariachi band, even if such a thing exists."

"What are we going to have then?"

Shay shrugged. "Still figuring that out since you're not

being helpful at all. It's November, and we're not getting married until the summer. We've got plenty of time to figure this out. It's not like the world's going to end before then."

James grunted. "If it did, it'd make things simpler."

"Don't go cheering for the end of the world because you want to get out of wedding planning."

---

The next morning, James finished brushing his teeth and stepped out of the bathroom. After a little fun with Shay, he'd gone to bed early, so he felt extra-refreshed.

*Maybe another level four will pop up this afternoon and I can beat their ass down.*

Shay sat up in bed and stretched. "You got somewhere you need to run off to early today?"

"I figured I'd take Thomas for a walk." James headed to his closet to pull out some jeans and a t-shirt. He tossed them on the edge of the bed. "I don't know if he's getting enough exercise, especially with all that food he's been eating. I've been thinking about installing an auto-launching frisbee system in the back so he can entertain himself when I'm inside. Or maybe some sort of pop-up bounty he can tackle."

"Oh, he's fine." Shay furrowed her brow and pointed to his finger. "You still have that tape on your finger? I thought you told me you were going to use Whispy to take care of that before you went to bed last night."

"I had other shit to handle, and I didn't want to deal with him bitching before I went to sleep and putting me in a bad mood." James held up his finger. No blood had seeped out from underneath the tape.

"It doesn't hurt at all?" Shay asked. "It's not like you wore Whispy yesterday."

James stared at his finger. The digit had been a little sore the previous night, but now there was no pain. "Nope. It doesn't hurt at all."

"Huh." When James started pulling the tape off, there was still no pain. When he finally yanked the last piece off, the underlying skin was pale, but there was no sign he'd ever been injured. Not even a scratch. "I didn't expect that shit."

Shay crawled toward him on the bed, her eyes narrowing. "I thought you said it was a pretty deep cut?"

"It was." James peered at his unwounded finger. "If I didn't use Whispy, I'd need stitches or a potion."

"And you were more obsessed with your sauce preparation than first aid?"

"Got to have priorities in life."

Shay hopped off the bed and walked over to James, grabbing his hand and turning it back and forth. "Fuck. It's completely healed. I mean, it's one thing when you're wearing Whispy, even when he's in his rest mode shit, but you didn't even use him this time."

"It's no big deal." James grunted. "People heal even without alien amulets."

"They don't nearly slice off their fingers and heal overnight without one of those or magic." Shay released his hand. "Did he tell you he was going to do this kind of thing to you?"

"You have to understand: he tells me shit, but it's not

always clear what he means." James shrugged and dropped his hand. "And talking to him is like talking to a bitchy computer with a fucking mind of its own. He only cares about me getting tougher and the primary directives."

"The mutually conflicting ones?"

"Yeah."

Shay frowned. "But he's told you about alterations he's going to do. You'd think he would have mentioned that you could heal a lot quicker even without him."

James nodded. "I think he can only do so much if I don't want it. That's probably why he needed to be able to talk to me. To get a lot of this shit working to begin with."

Shay sat down on the edge of the bed and crossed her legs, the bottom of her nightgown riding up slightly. "He didn't ask for permission when he basically turned you from a Vax to a human. I mean, you're human enough for basic human DNA tests to work on you. That's a pretty fucking major change."

"I was a little kid, and he had just been turned on." James grabbed his jeans and started pulling them on. "As far as he was concerned, it was an emergency, but I'm older now, and he doesn't have control over me even though he's supposed to. I'm supposed to just be his meat puppet where he's doing all the shot-calling, but that shit didn't work out for him. I know it pisses him off that he's not in charge, but he gets that if he doesn't do what I say, he'll be shit out of luck."

"But if he's changed you to the point that you have accelerated healing even without wearing him, I wonder how far he can push you now that you're more in sync."

"A lot fucking further." James buttoned his jeans. "If I'm

supposed to be able to hold on out a planet by myself for a while before reinforcements show up, that means shit like near-complete regeneration without magical potions and not needing magic."

Shay's face twitched. "But that thing's powered normally by hate and anger."

"Yeah. So? That's not a big mystery."

"And the whole magic-powering-it thing *we* figured out, and from what the Alliance assholes have said, magic isn't common in the galaxy." Shay frowned.

James nodded. "Not following you."

"Does that mean that if Whispy was in control, he'd keep you on a rage drip all the time?"

James frowned and thought it over. "But he can't directly piss me off. He tells me to do shit, but it's not like he floods my mind with anger and hatred or whatever."

"Maybe he could have when you were younger," Shay replied. "Did you ever use it when you were a kid? After you got to Earth?"

James shook his head. "Nope. I didn't even have it for the longest time, and when the priests finally gave it back to me, I didn't want to wear it. I couldn't remember every-thing from when I was younger, but I knew I didn't trust that fucking amulet for some reason. For a long time, I thought it was cursed. I even talked to Father McCartney about that, but he told me it was just a piece of jewelry. He didn't force me to wear it."

"And the first time you wore it? What happened then?"

"I freaked the fuck out, but I also realized what it did: made me tougher and stronger." James stared at the amulet sitting on his nightstand. "I understood what I could do with it, but I still thought it was cursed. I wondered if I should go talk to Father McCartney about it, but I decided against it."

Shay gave him a shallow nod. "Why?"

"Because I didn't want him to kick me out. I started thinking that if I have this cursed amulet, maybe it's not just that I have it because I'm a bad person, but what if I were demonic or some shit like that?"

Shay winced. "Geeze."

"After a while, I figured it didn't matter." James shrugged. "I figured if I did enough good and only used it when I had to deal with evil assholes, it wouldn't matter. Even if it was a little evil, God would forgive me." He let out a dark chuckle. "Not sure if it's evil or not because it's alien and not demonic, but if I can use it to beat down psycho assholes, I'm gonna continue using it."

"I'm not one to say anything about people being good or evil," Shay replied quietly. "I spent most of my adult life as a cold-blooded killer, but I will tell you, the one thing I learned during that time is that any weapon, no matter how fancy, is just a tool in the end, and good or evil usually has a lot more to do with who is on the receiving end."

James grunted and slipped on the t-shirt. "I know. I don't let this shit worry me much. Whispy's gonna do his thing, and he hasn't done anything that makes my life more complicated than it was before. Everyone else has done *that*." He grabbed some socks from his dresser and started rolling them on. "And sometimes you just need to kick some fucking ass to make your point."

Shay chuckled. "I don't disagree, James. I think even without the Whispy stuff, between your barbeque crap, my teaching, and the wedding, we've got plenty to keep us busy. It might just be that the amulet ends up changing you and it accomplishes nothing more than you being able to party for a few more hours during our reception."

James stared at Shay, an idea percolating in his head.

Shay looked back at him, confused. "What?"

"We should invite the top local mobsters to our wedding."

Shay blinked. "What did you just say? It sounded like you said we should invite the top mobsters to our wedding?"

"Yeah," James responded. "The more I think about it, the better the idea sounds."

"Why the fuck would you want to do that?"

"My wedding's gonna take all our guys off the streets. I don't want people getting ideas."

Shay sighed. "It's just a wedding, and the cops will still be around."

James grunted. "I don't want them to have to deal with shit while we're getting married. If we have the top local pieces of shit around, they'll tell their boys to keep an eye on things because they don't want to risk pissing me off on what's supposed to be the happiest day of my fucking life."

Shay snort-laughed. "Are you basically saying you want to invite the heads of the local mobs to effectively hold them hostage at *our wedding*?"

"Yeah. Why the fuck not?" James grinned. "That shit will be funny."

CHAPTER ELEVEN

Shay pulled out of the college parking in her new Porsche, humming under her breath. She preferred her Fiat Spider, but it was nice to mix up her rides every now and again. She snickered as she remembered the old days and how she needed to explain away driving expensive sports cars on a part-time professor's salary.

Now it was easy. Anytime she had anything expensive, she just attributed it to a gift from James. Everyone in the world knew how rich he was, and they just assumed he was a very generous fiancé.

Her phone rang. She glanced down at her console display; her phone was already interfaced with her car.

"Smite-Williams?" Shay muttered. She hadn't been expecting contact from him, but she answered the call on speakerphone. "What's up, Professor?"

"Good evening, Miz Carson," he responded, his voice full of cheer, as always. "I'd like you to stop by as soon as possible so we could discuss a big job. It's rather time-sensitive, so I'd really appreciate it if you could stop by tonight to discuss it."

Shay sighed. "I appreciate the call, but the timing is shit on this. You know I'm teaching this semester. I can't just drop everything and go on a raid. Maybe something during winter vacation?"

Smite-Williams laughed. "Aye, I understand your new schedule, but you forget: you might be *a* professor, but I'm *the Professor.*"

Shay frowned as she turned onto the street and joined the dense flow of rush-hour traffic. "And what the hell does that mean in this particular context? I don't have time for this Father O'Banion shit."

The Professor's laughter faded to a chuckle. "It means, Miz Carson, that I share the same day job as you, and I also understand the relevant schedule. The job I have in mind shouldn't be a lengthy one, provided you see to it quickly, and you have a nice Thanksgiving vacation coming up in mere days."

"No turkey, only bullets, blood, and artifacts?"

"Aye. There might be turkeys where you're going. I can't guarantee there won't be."

Shay sighed. "Okay. Whatever. Let me text James to let him know I'll be late, and I'll be right over."

"Thank you. That's all I can ask." He hung up.

*I hope I don't end up regretting this,* she thought darkly.

<hr>

Shay settled in across from the Professor after glancing over her shoulder and surveying the room for anyone who looked to be out of place. There were several men and women who didn't seem to be having a good time, which made them suspicious at the Leanan Sidhe. The raucous atmosphere always seemed to intoxicate people even without the beer, and only people with something to hide, like Shay, didn't give in to that atmosphere.

*High-priority jobs mean big risks. Better be careful the next few days even if I don't end up taking the job.*

Shay finished her check of the room. None of the potential hostiles spared even the smallest glance her way. That didn't mean she was safe, but it did cut down on the likely risk.

"I'm here," Shay commented. "So what's the big job that I had to run over here to discuss tonight?"

The Professor didn't answer at first, instead taking a huge gulp of his beer. "You've previously recovered artifacts related to a vimana for me. Quite successfully, I might add."

Shay nodded. "Yeah. What about it? From what you told me before, you made it sound like you had a magical flying fortress stashed in a lake somewhere. You ready to buzz the Eiffel Tower with it?"

"Hidden in a lake? I *did* give that impression, didn't I?" A merry smile followed.

Shay rolled her eyes. "Why bullshit me?"

"It can be useful to keep people off-guard. You, of all people, should understand that, Miz Carson."

"Just tell me. Do you or do you not have a vimana? I'm here for a job offer, not games."

"Aye, but games are so fun." The Professor sighed. "To offer complete honesty, no, I don't actually have a vimana, small or large, parked anywhere, and now I'm interested in the ultimate prize, an actual vimana. In this case, it's exactly as you described: a massive flying fortress powered by magic. It has likely not been in operation since the last time the gates opened. Even with the gates open, it still will require a huge amount of magic to be fed into it to get it to operate, and it will only be a shadow of what it could be at full capacity."

Shay furrowed her brow. "So, wait, you want me to go on a tomb raid to get a magical flying castle that you admit is huge and is going to need shitloads of magic to even work? How the hell am I supposed to pull that off? My pockets aren't that big."

The Professor chuckled. "That would be impressive, but no, I'm not asking you to stick the vimana in your pocket or backpack. Technically it's not the vimana you'll be recovering, which is why this is a practical job offer."

"Another activation artifact? Some sort of magical fuel cell?"

"Far simpler, yet more important." The Professor grinned. "You'll be recovering a map artifact that points to the current location of the vimana. I'm sure there will be some confusion based on how old the map is, but you don't have to worry about that. I have other people to help with the final collection and launching of the vimana. It might be fine in its current location, but it's important that we know where it is and have firm control of it as a future asset.

"I should be able to fit a map in my backpack," Shay replied with a smirk. "Do I need to take any special precautions?"

The Professor shook his head. "No. I should note it's a small glass sphere rather than the paper kind, just to be clear, but it'll lead me to the vimana all the same."

"And why do you even need a vimana?" Shay asked.

The Professor looked more amused than offended. "Worried I'll try to pull a *Gulliver's Travels?*"

Shay snorted. "When I first heard of a vimana, I was thinking magical plane, and you immediately upgraded it to a magical castle, and now we're all the way up to city? Maybe I *should* be worried."

"Ah, Miz Carson, I assure you that it's nothing quite so grand." The Professor's easy smile remained on his face. "It's just interesting that you now care so much. You've rarely expressed that much concern about what I might do with an artifact. I'm curious if this means you now don't trust me."

"I don't trust anyone on this planet except Alison and James, and she's a teen who can be tricked, and James can be a little too honest for his own good." Shay matched Smite-Williams' smile with a predatory one of her own. "It's not that I think you're ready to go all Rhazdon, Professor. I just care a little more about the future now, so it doesn't hurt to ask."

In a rare moment, the smile vanished from the man's face briefly as he picked up his beer and took another drink. His cheer, fake or not, returned after he downed more of the dark liquid.

The Professor set his glass down. "Two things motivate me in this particular case, Miz Carson." He held up one finger. "Firstly, when it comes to weapons, denying them to your enemy is sometimes as important as having them yourself, but how can we deny them to an enemy if we don't even know where they are?"

Shay nodded. "Fair enough."

The Professor held up another finger. "Secondly, one could make the argument that recent events have suggested that having a magical flying fortress available might be useful if one had to deal with unusual threats. This isn't just any random vimana. It's one of the more powerful ones from the previous times, and it's my belief, along with that of a few others, that we could potentially get it into space."

Shay stared at the Professor, frowning. "How openly can I speak?"

"As honestly as you want, Miz Carson." The Professor gestured around the room. "There's a reason I like this location so much. The entire CIA could try to spy on us but fail."

"Recent events," Shay echoed. "You mean that alien shit?"

"Certain mutual acquaintances in the government feel that we need more resources at our disposal." The Professor mimicked an explosion with his hand. "I believe the exact wording was, 'What do we do if some asshole alien decides to drop ten anti-matter torpedoes on a city from orbit?'"

Shay snorted. "Not so trusting of the Alliance, after all?"

"Aye, and even the lad can only do so much from the ground." The Professor's brow lifted. "Everything we know about our new diplomatic friends suggests that magic is their Achilles' heel, so it doesn't hurt to collect a few extra-powerful magical trinkets. Unfortunately, when the gates opened, such old-school technology quests as advanced space travel became secondary concerns.

"It's only recently that people have begun looking back into that and giving it decent funding." He shook his head. "We might be able to send a few people into space on rockets, but it's not like Earth can field a fleet of spaceships, let alone warships, and Earth's magic grows weaker the farther you go from the planet. Some of the portal experiments NASA has been trying to prove that. Also, the Oricerans are leery of most strategic-level magics. It's unclear whether they'd be capable of shooting a ship out of orbit with magic, or even willing to try to do so."

Shay frowned. "You telling me they'd let an Earth city get nuked?"

"I think they've lived with mostly peace for centuries after a war that nearly destroyed their world, and they're not eager to get involved in a new planetary-scale war." The Professor polished off his drink and let out a satisfied sigh. "And in the end, this is our planet, not theirs, so it's up to us to defend it."

Shay folded her arms over her chest, still trying to take in the enormity of what was being discussed. It might be just another tomb raid for her, but she was being asked to help recover a map to a magical fortress in case the planet wanted to fight off an alien invasion.

*Things were a lot simpler when I didn't worry about anything but who I was killing for a living.*

"I want you to answer my one question as honestly as possible," Shay replied, her voice barely above a whisper. "Because I need to know what the fuck is going on before I get too involved."

The Professor held up his hand to tell her to wait. A waitress zoomed by, picked up his old glass, and set down a new one without even stopping.

"Go ahead, Miz Carson."

Shay lowered her arms and frowned. "Does the government have information that the Alliance is going to make another play for James?"

The Professor tilted his head, his eyes narrowing ever so slightly. "You'd try to make him run, wouldn't you?"

Shay locked eyes with the older man. "I'm not gonna let him walk into a fight he can't win. He's getting stronger, but he's still a long way from whatever they think he is."

"And, what, you'd choose him over the world?"

Shay barked out a harsh laugh. "All this time and you still don't get me, do you, Smite-Williams?"

"Please explain it to me then," the Professor replied.

"I'm not a good person. Just because I stopped killing people for money doesn't mean I'm a good person. Just because I love Alison and James doesn't make me a good person."

"I see."

Shay shook her head. "No, you don't. The rest of the world can burn. I'm not letting James sacrifice himself for it."

The Professor offered her a disarming smile. "And no one is suggesting that you do so, Miz Carson. If you will recall, Senator Johnston all but offered to go to war on the lad's behalf."

"I just wanted to make sure we understood each other."

"We understand each other." The Professor nodded. "Which is all the more reason for you to help me locate the vimana. The more tools we have available, the less anyone will worry about what one individual man, however unbelievable and impressive, can bring to the fight. And no, I don't know of any current particular threats, but you know what I say. If you want peace, prepare for war."

Shay took a few deep breaths to try to calm her pounding heart.

*Shit. Where did that come from? Is that why I've been so obsessed with James training the symbiont more? Because I'm worried the assholes are coming for him?*

"Fine," Shay spat. "Let's prepare for war. Maybe these assholes have the long view and will wait a hundred years, but how do you know if this thing still works? It's been thousands of years, and you don't even know where it is, so it's not like there was some vimana inspector checking on it every few centuries to top off the magical gas tank."

"Aye," the Professor replied. "But the energy signature of a viable vimana can be detected if you know what to look for, and a helpful elf did just that in this particular case."

"Why the hell do you need me to find a map, then? Why not just track that shit directly and cut out the tomb raider in the middle? It's not like I mind the money, but it seems like a waste of time."

The Professor gave her a condescending look that made her want to headbutt him. "We've tried that already. Direct tracking fails; whether from residual magic on the vimana or something else, we can't say. It might just be the low levels of magic involved. Think of it like detecting trace amounts of some compound on Earth in the atmosphere. You might know a chemical is being released, but you can't easily pinpoint it. But in this case, I do know where the map is: on a remote island east of Tanzania in ruins that belonged to the Kilwa Sultanate."

*The elf? Probably the Fixer. He's been involved with this alien shit from the beginning. Once again that lazy elf is making me do all the hard work with all his fucking excuses.*

"Okay." Shay nodded. "This is starting to sound like a decent job."

"Isn't it, though?" The Professor ran his tongue along the inside of his cheek. "Unfortunately, it's not as simple as going to the island, which, incidentally, is occasionally used as a base by local rebels."

"I'm not worried about the local AK boys, but if they're incidental, then who is the main threat?" Shay frowned. This job was becoming more complicated than she had expected.

"We both know you've dealt with certain men interested in alien objects. Just because you've eliminated some of those men doesn't mean that the ones who employed them are all gone."

Shay groaned. "Are you fucking kidding me? More black ops rogue government assholes? This shit's even more annoying than I thought. Can't Johnston do something about them?"

"Trust me, Miz Carson, he is. I'm not privy to everything he is doing or planning, but he's already putting in efforts to minimize the risk to you. That said, it might not hurt to bring the lad along, and let me make it clear. No one, including our mutual employer, is going to lose sleep if you're forced to repel them through lethal means."

*James has been kind of annoyed about Alison not coming*

*home for break. He had his fun at his bounty the other day, but a tomb raid might further take his mind off shit.*

Shay shrugged. "A little ass-kicking always brings a smile to his face."

The Professor clapped once and rubbed his hands together. "Good. I'll send along the information. Just be cautious. These people aren't just ruthless like the mercenaries and tomb raiders you're used to dealing with. They have access to advanced technology, and it's my understanding that they have no problem killing even innocent people, let alone hired tomb raiders."

"Good. Both James and I could use a good workout."

## CHAPTER TWELVE

*You've got to be fucking kidding me,* Shay thought.

She frowned as she glanced into her rearview camera. There was nothing more insulting than someone following her and not even bothering to pretend they weren't. She expected a certain professional courtesy from anyone who might be planning to kill her.

*Just because I don't always practice defensive seating doesn't mean I don't check for assholes following me right after a sensitive meeting. Or do you really think you're that slick? Were those assholes I spotted earlier exactly what I worried about?*

Another quick check in her mirrors and camera reinforced her initial belief. A black sedan with tinted windows and two drones were following her. Given the conversation she'd just had with Smite-Williams, she doubted her newfound friends were something as harmless as paparazzi or mobsters.

*You assholes are really underestimating me, and this is gonna end badly for you because of it.*

Shay changed lanes and took a hard right to verify the

tail. A few seconds later, the car careened around the corner, and the drones followed right above it.

*Thanks for the warning, Professor. These guys showed up even earlier than you thought, I bet. Everyone's eager, huh?*

*If these assholes are from Ragnarök or Nephilim, they aren't going to want to take me too publicly, but if I go to the police, they might end up killing someone. Shit, they might even do it and try to frame me. With my background, digging out of that might take a while.*

*Of course, they have to come at me when I'm not in the car loaded down with all the toys. Fuckers. How inconsiderate can you be? You should never attack a woman when she doesn't have her magic sword with her. It's just rude.*

Shay had her gnome-crafted knives, which was something, even if they lacked the full anti-magic penetration of her *tachi*. She'd been pleasantly surprised by how effective they could be in the absence of the sword. In the end, it didn't matter how cool she looked when she killed her enemies, just that she defeated them.

"Fuck it," she muttered. Shay would need to end the encounter as quickly as possible. If the assholes wanted to party, she'd show them why it was a mistake to invite her. There was always the small possibility they were something as boring as surviving Harriken, cartel members, or someone else from one of the organizations or groups she had helped demolish in the last few years despite the extra hardware and timing.

*Could they just be overly well-equipped mob carjackers? The two drones are a bit much, but everyone's upping their game these days.*

*Doesn't much matter. I might as well end this shit.*

Shay yanked the Porsche into a narrow alley. The tires screeched with her hard stop. With a quick press of her thumb against a biometric sensor, she popped open a hidden compartment under her seat and pulled out a couple of sonic grenades, a flashbang, and some extra magazines. She stuffed the deadly treasure into her jacket pockets.

A drone zoomed overhead and continued past her.

*Where did the other drone go? They up to something?*

Shay fingered the jade ring and pendant, again appreciating James' wisdom in his choice of engagement ring and present, even if they still needed to figure out the wedding ring situation. Good defenses could keep her alive, even in an ambush situation where she lacked her best equipment. She activated the defensive artifacts before pulling out her gun and throwing open her door.

Loud buzzing from the back end of the alley caught her attention.

*What the fuck was that? It sounded like an EMP. But why?*

Shay looked at her car. Her Porsche was still on, and it wasn't hardened against electrical attacks. Her watch was fine as well. The EMP hadn't been aimed into the alley.

*Directional EMP, then?*

A long horn blast sounded, along with an echoing crash. The grinding of metal on metal echoed down the alley. The cab of an 18-wheeler rolled past the back end of the alley with blood on the windshield. The trailer scraped across the asphalt a few seconds later, sparks marking its path as it ended up blocking the alley.

Shay stared at the wreck. She'd fought lizardmen in Romania not all that long ago, and she'd felt less surprise.

"Did these fuckers just cause a truck crash to block me in?"

Movement and the squeal of a driver riding his brakes too hard brought her attention back to the front of the alley. The black sedan from before now blocked the head of the alley.

Shay was pinned on both sides. There would be no avoiding a confrontation.

The sedan's doors opened, and four suited men stepped out, each carrying what looked like a dark wooden flintlock pistol with glowing yellow glyphs on the barrel.

*Huh. Hard to tell from this far away, but those look more like magic than alien tech. That I can handle. Again, these assholes are underestimating me. These fuckers are gonna pay for coming after me. I don't care if they are secret government assassins.*

The men all aimed at the Porsche. Shay crouched behind her door, mostly to keep the slight argent sheen from her defensive artifacts out of sight. Whatever surprise she could manage might help. She hadn't seen either drone since the truck crash, and if they were too high, they would have trouble picking out fine details about her skin.

"This doesn't have to be unpleasant," shouted one of the men, an unassuming specimen except for his dark suit and the odd gun. "Or at least any more unpleasant."

"I'm not the one who just killed some random trucker to make a roadblock," Shay called back. "We've already gone past unpleasant, but don't you think that was kind of an idiotic move? What are you going to do, gun down all the local police? Haven't you heard the song, Captain Flintlock? You only get one shot."

The man chuckled. "I assure you that these have a lot more than one shot."

"What can I say? *Hamilton* lied to me. Maybe James is onto something about musicals sucking, but you've made a big fucking mistake anyway."

Captain Flintlock murmured something to one of the men beside him before turning his head back toward Shay. "If you come with us right away, you won't be harmed. If you resist, you very well may be, but in either event, you're not leaving here unless it's in our custody, dead or alive."

Shay scoffed. "Let's just say your track record doesn't make me trust you, asshole, and the only reason I haven't killed you all is that I want to know who the hell you are before I do. It's important to know who to target for revenge."

"You don't need to know that information at this time. You just need to know that you come with us alive, or you can die here in an alley and come with us anyway. And let me be clear, Miss Carson…this time you'll actually *be* dead, unlike that little stunt you pulled back East. We're a whole different level of threat than what you're used to dealing with."

*Fuck. Between the weapons, the attitude, and the info, they have to be government. Who exactly works for Nephilim and Ragnarök in the government? DoD civilians? Hidden office FBI? CIA? Guess it doesn't matter. I'll kill them and grab one of their phones. Peyton can figure everything else out from them. Time to remind them who they're dealing with.*

*Shit. Peyton.*

Shay pulled out her phone. She had no signal despite

being in the middle of one of the largest cities in the United States.

*Fucking government jamming. Pussies.*

"So what's it going to be, Miss Carson?" asked Captain Flintlock.

Shay laughed. "If you know who I really am, then you know how many people I've put down, magicals and non-magicals, and I wasn't as well-equipped back in the day. You looking to die, asshole?"

"Oh, we're quite aware of your penchant for high-powered artifacts and weapons," Captain Flintlock replied. "Don't worry. We've brought just the weapons we need to get through your defenses. Oh, and if you think the police or AET will show up, you're mistaken. We've taken measures to assure that their arrival will be delayed. No one's coming to help you. Not the police, not any of your little friends."

"I noticed the jamming already. Good. Thanks. It means I can kill you without having to answer a lot of questions." Shay crept backward, keeping the door between her and the men. "And you guys are fucking morons. If you knew enough to show up with not one but *four* special guns, you should have been smart enough to know not to fuck with me to begin with." She primed and arced the sonic grenade over the door.

The men opened fire. Hissing, the flintlocks spit tight balls of blue-black fire that blasted straight through her door and narrowly missed her. Shay scrambled behind the car as they continued blowing holes in her car. Her sonic grenade lay on the ground, and all four men still stood there not even a hint they were bothered.

*Some sort of shields, then. Too bad shit couldn't be easier, but they've ruined this perfectly good car. They're just lucky it's not my Fiat.*

Shay wasn't sure if her artifacts could hold up to their weapons, but in any case, she wasn't James. If they could get through her shields, there was no alien amulet to stitch her back together if she lost consciousness.

*Okay, let's play this smart. First I need to test their defenses.*

Shay popped up to fire a few rounds at Captain Flintlock and the man closest to him. Her bullets bounced off invisible fields around the men, and she ducked back down as their flintlock fireballs ripped right through the windshield. The hiss of the firing continued, but no rounds penetrated through the back of the Porsche.

*So they can't blast through everything? That's nice, but it doesn't do me any good when I can't get through their shields.*

Shay rolled to the side to fire off several more rounds, but the new angle didn't help her hurt the men either.

The Flintlock Brigade ceased fire. The two drones buzzed overhead as they appeared from over one of the buildings and circled the area.

"Are you ready to end this farce, Miss Carson?" called Captain Flintlock. "You have to appreciate now that we've taken all necessary measures to deal with you. We don't want to have to kill you, but we will. I'm not going to guarantee you'll survive this, but if you come with us, at least you'll have a chance."

*Time for test number two.*

Shay holstered her pistol and readied one of her gnome-crafted knives. She shot up for a quick toss at Captain Flintlock.

The suited assassin didn't flinch at her throw. His eyes widened as the knife pierced his shield and closed on his face. The magic slowed the blade, but the point jabbed his cheek, drawing blood before the knife fell to the ground, scraping his jaw.

*Not total anti-magic, but good enough.*

Shay rolled back around the car as the flintlocks came alive again, blowing holes through the other side of the car. She needed to close on the men to finish them off, but there was no way she could close without getting ventilated.

She gritted her teeth and pulled out another sonic grenade in one hand and a flashbang in the other. She tossed the sonic over the car as a distraction, waited one second, then threw the flashbang, popping up immediately after the echoing boom. The men groaned.

*There's always a weakness to exploit. You idiots just assumed I threw two sonics.*

Shay yanked out another knife as she charged toward the men who were clutching their eyes and firing wildly, blasting holes in the ground and nearby walls, knocking asphalt and concrete shards into the air.

The angry woman closed the distance in seconds and shoved her knife against Captain Flintlock's throat, pushing with both hands through the thick field blocking her. It felt like trying to stab a man at the bottom of a bowl of thick molasses.

The force was enough to ensure her blade pierced his throat. He gurgled as blood leaked out of his mouth. His gun fell to the ground as his fingers twitched.

Shay dropped and grabbed the magical firearm. She

jerked to her side and fired at another man. His shield took the first hit, but the second tunneled right through his heart. The third man died as she added a new hole to his head, and the fourth man had just gotten his sight back in time to see her kill him.

*Nothing more satisfying than killing people with their own weapons.*

Several more cars and vans screeched to a halt down the street. More suited men with rifles rushing out and ducking behind the opened doors. They popped out their magazines and slapped in new ones.

*Shit, those are probably anti-magics if they're bothering to change.*

Shay looked up at the two circling drones and nailed them both with the flintlock before rushing back toward her car. The new arrivals opened fire, their bullet storm riddling the sedan with dozens of holes.

*Well, shit. They've got me pinned even if I've got the Ultimate Flintlock of Rogue Government Operative Killing or whatever.*

Shay peeked around the corner to fire, but the intense suppression fire from the reinforcements forced her back into the alley. Shouts and footfalls grew closer.

*Fuck.*

Two large tactical drones descended from overhead, both carrying large rockets.

*More drones?*

Shay narrowed her eyes. Her defenses could take a hit from a rocket or two—not that she'd tested that exact scenario, but she was pretty sure.

*James, if your engagement ring can't even take a rocket, I swear I'm gonna come back and haunt all your ribs.*

She lifted her flintlock, but the drones zoomed out of the alley, releasing their rockets toward the reinforcements. The area shook with thunderous explosions, and something flashed from behind her.

*What the fuck?*

Shay spun that way. A massive rope of light wrapped around the trailer and yanked on it, slowly pulling it away from the alley.

A hail of bullets shredded one of the drones, and it tumbled to the ground. The other released its final rocket before bullets struck its rotors, and the machine plummeted to the hard asphalt below.

"Come on, Shay!" shouted a man's voice from the other end of the alley. It sounded familiar, but she couldn't put a name to the voice.

The light rope vanished, and although it hadn't moved the trailer much, there was more than enough room for her to get through.

Shay sprinted that way, the flintlock still in hand and ready. She raised the weapon, ready to fire.

A handsome dark-haired man in a suit stood just outside the back end of the alley.

Shay snorted. "Switched to contacts, Daniel?"

It'd been a long time since she had last talked to the CIA agent. His presence there and his help suggested the men after her were CIA from a different faction, given what little she knew about his true background.

A blonde Light Elf in a leather catsuit stood next to him.

Shay raised an eyebrow. "You join some BDSM club since the last time we talked?"

Daisy laughed. "I like her."

"We don't have time for jokes." Daniel whipped out his pistol, a small silver model with a barrel far too small to fit a bullet. He pulled the trigger, and a bright blue beam shot out. A man screamed from the front of the alley. "We can chat later, Professor Carson, or Aletheia, whichever you prefer." He nodded to a nearby silver Jaguar. "For now, let's get the hell out of here."

Shay sighed and glanced over her shoulder at her brand-new hole-riddled Porsche.

CHAPTER THIRTEEN

The Jaguar screamed down the mostly empty streets. Daniel pressed a few buttons on the touchscreen labeled Chromatic Active Camouflage. The system beeped, and a confirmation message appeared.

*I'm having car envy here*, Shay thought. *The guy does have some nice toys. I'll have to give him that, even if he is a government stooge. And he did help me back there.*

Shay glanced at the elf in the backseat. "By the way, who the hell are you? I don't remember seeing you around CIA Boy before. Then again, I didn't get to meet any of his friends."

The elf gave Shay a pleasant smile. "I'm Daisy."

"Daisy, huh?" Shay arched a brow. "And you're in the CIA? Do they even allow elves in the CIA?"

"I'm not in the CIA." The elf shook her head and made a pained face.

Shay eyed her. "You're not in the CIA? You just hang out with a CIA agent and help him take on other government agents?"

"Yes. Being in the CIA would be painful and far too boring. Just think of me as a freelancer who let Daniel convince me to help him out for far longer than I should have with this really corny speech about... You know what? I don't even remember. Something like, 'Do you want to do pointless mercenary jobs for the rest of your life or save the two worlds?'"

Daniel snorted. "I don't think I phrased it that way, but that speech was pretty good. It got me a whole team of qualified operatives and support personnel."

"Sure, it worked. I'm still here, aren't I?" Daisy winked. "Though how much of that is the speech versus other things?"

Daniel frowned and cleared his throat.

Shay chuckled. "Just so you know, that speech wouldn't have worked on me. It's hard to appeal to a sense of altruism if it doesn't exist."

"I still recruited you, just in a different way." Daniel tapped a few buttons, and multiple camera views appeared on his console display. "Altruism works for some people, challenge for others. Ego for some."

Shay sighed. "Anyway, thanks for the assist, Agent Goldstein, even if it's been a while. I had those guys on the ropes, but I don't mind them all checking out sooner."

"Winters," Daniel replied.

"Summers?" Shay offered, confused by the sudden seasonal reference.

"No, Winters. It's my actual last name," Daniel explained. "But just call me Daniel. I think we're well past the point of bullshit excuses and lies about what and who we truly are. I know all about who you are, Professor

Carson. You're Aletheia, one of the most skilled tomb raiders on the planet. You're also a retired professional killer, who was also one of the most skilled on the planet. You faked your death to escape a cartel hunting you, a cartel whose entire top leadership was conveniently destroyed shortly after James Brownstone, and I presume you, traveled to the same area where they were having a meeting."

Shay grinned. "Coincidences happen. Bad coincidences happen more often to bad people. And those cartel guys were very, very bad people."

Daisy eyed Shay, surprise and respect on her face. "The two of you killed a cartel?"

Shay shrugged. "To be fair, there were a lot of explosive drones involved. I forgot how many each of us individually killed. You'd have to ask James."

"Impressive." Daisy gave a quick nod.

Shay shrugged. "To be clear, I didn't do it because I was trying to be a hero. Again, no altruism. I did it because the assholes had a hit out on me." She turned back to Daniel. "If you know all that, it makes this easier for both of us. Is that why you basically disappeared? You didn't want some dangerous killer dirtying up your black ops? And call me Shay. Only my students call me Professor Carson, and occasionally my department head, when I make him."

"It had nothing to do with you and everything to do with my group and our operations." Daniel sighed. "Things were getting too hot. I was honest with you before about everything I told you. I'm part of a special group in the CIA dedicated to alien matters, but my group isn't the only one, even if we're currently the ones calling the shots. My group has a little different attitude than Fortis. They were the ones mostly calling the shots before. They had the approval until not all that long ago of the highest levels of government, and they used it for ruthless actions."

"Fortis? They were the flintlock brigade that tried to kill me back there?" Shay lifted the weapon and grinned. "I earned a really nice trophy. It almost makes it worth it to have them try to kill me."

Daniel glanced at the weapon. "Don't get too attached. I'm surprised you still have it. Any second now, you won't."

Shay scoffed. "I'm not giving this back, Daniel. Those Fortis assholes just murdered my new Porsche, and this is my compensation." The flintlock cracked and turned to dust. "What the hell did you do, Daniel?"

*I swear, if this guy is fucking with me, he's not gonna like how I react. Gratitude only goes so far.*

"It wasn't me," The agent offered with a smirk. "Those things are powered by this kind of central battery, which is large and unwieldy. They probably had it in the trunk of the car. You get too far away and…well, you saw. It makes the flintlocks not all that handy for field work, not that there were a huge number of them to begin with."

"Damn it," Shay grumbled. "So now I'm out a Porsche *and* a cool new gun."

Daisy snickered. Shay glared at her.

The elf held up a hand. "Not trying to be a bitch. Trust me, Shay. I've been there. So has Daniel. Fortis trying to kill us is practically a daily pastime for some agents."

Shay dropped the remnants on the floor mat and dusted her hands. "Well, this has just been a shit night, now, hasn't it?"

Daniel was staring straight ahead, his brow furrowed.

"Thanks, Ronni," he muttered under his breath. "Just let me know if they're coming our way. Between Shay and what the drones did, we took down a lot. That should at least give them a reason to pause for a day or two and reconsider their tactics."

Shay looked back to Daisy. "Some sort of hidden receiver?"

The elf nodded. "Ronni's one of our tech support people. Very creative sort."

*They aren't set up so differently than Peyton and me or James and Heather. A few fancier gadgets here and there, and probably more backup, but same principle.*

Daniel sighed and looked at Shay. "Our drone coverage suggests that no one from Fortis is following us. I'm surprised they were so bold. Going after you in the middle of the city like that was risky, even with them taking measures to make sure the police didn't come. That must mean they're very worried about you finishing the job."

Shay leaned back in her seat and got comfortable. "So these Fortis assholes are, what, the guys behind Projects Ragnarök and Nephilim? They're the guys hiring people like Durand?"

Daniel nodded. "Among other things. Originally, they were a secret group tasked with investigating and controlling non-Oriceran alien activity on Earth, but their method for doing this boiled down to taking whatever artifacts they could find and killing anyone who had seen too much."

"Including an entire town," Shay muttered. "Nice guys.

Glad to see the government is looking out for the little guy."

Daniel glanced her way, surprise on his face. "You knew about that?"

Daisy whistled. "Impressive."

"I suspected," Shay explained. "More accurately, my main support guy suspected, but I don't get it. Why you being so forthright all of a sudden?"

Daniel's expression turned grim. "First of all, let me make it damned clear that I don't approve of their tactics. I've been opposing them for a while, and helping you back there was just part of that. Second, I'm being this honest because we no longer have the luxury of playing games, and since I now understand who and what you are, including your capabilities, I don't see the point of pretending otherwise. I know about the job you have, and I know how important it is to non-Fortis people in the government."

Shay frowned. "We need to clear something up, since we're being honest. Are these Fortis assholes after me because of you?"

The Professor's warning remained in the back of her mind, but she wanted to make sure it wasn't a coincidence and that she hadn't been dragged into some mess by Daniel and Daisy.

The agent shook his head. "We've been putting extra effort into monitoring Fortis activity because we were told you were going to recover a map to a vimana that people above our paygrades who *aren't* ruthless psychos need in case shit gets out of control. This is the kind of thing we should have been concentrating on for years, instead of

Fortis going around murdering people and going all Men in Black on whatever aliens they could locate."

Daisy cleared her throat. "If we're being honest, there's no point in stopping at half-truths."

Shay shot him a dirty glance. "Yeah, Daniel."

Daniel frowned, his gaze flicking to the rearview mirror for a brief second. "Fortis is after you because of your connection to James Brownstone, and because they've been watching Smite-Williams to see who he might hire, but we did have an additional reason to suspect they'd be more active and able to send dedicated resources against you."

"And what would that be?" Shay asked.

"There was a recent incident during a CIA mission in East Asia. Two groups of agents allegedly died in a plane crash, although the reason still remains unclear. They're officially chalking it up to magical interference, but a lot of us don't believe that." Daniel's face tightened. "The CIA investigated it mostly as a counter-intelligence attack by a foreign government, but my group believes it was a cover by Fortis to disperse several of the remaining rogue operatives. In other words, Shay, they faked their deaths, just like you."

Shay snorted. "Hey, it's a useful tactic, rogue CIA or not."

Daisy chuckled quietly in the back. "Isn't rogue relative? It wasn't all that long ago that *we* were the rogue operatives, and Fortis were the guys with official backing."

Daniel shook his head. "Screw that. Fortis has killed innocent Americans. The CIA exists to protect Americans from foreign threats, terrestrial or extraterrestrial, not harm them. The minute Fortis agents decided they didn't care if they murdered people, they became unworthy of the Company, and they became unworthy of our country."

Shay kept quiet. She was more concerned that the Fortis agents had attempted to murder her, but Daniel did make a persuasive case. It just wasn't as if she felt any guilt about killing them. People who tried to kill her died. It was as simple as that, whether or not they were supposed to be the good guys.

"So are you two gonna help me with the vimana map job?" she asked.

Daniel's hands tightened around the wheel. "No. It's taking all our efforts to keep Fortis in check as it is. They're making some big plays right now, not just with the vimana, but also some other attempted assassinations and artifacts. We're stretched thin, and our assets, including Daisy and me, are best used to force them to disperse their resources, which means they have a worse chance of coming after you as you go for the map. We figure if we can at least restrict it to a trickle, you can handle them."

"Don't beat yourself up, Daniel. I'm a big girl. They happened to catch me at a bad time, and I still killed a bunch of them. If I'd had my favorite sword and a few other toys, it would have been over far quicker, let alone if James had been there." Shay groaned and scrubbed a hand down her face. "Shit, *James*. Are they going to fuck with him too?"

"I'll save you the trouble of a bunch of questions. Yes, we now know exactly what he is, and yes, so do they. After, the incident on the way to Vegas, all the top people in the alien circles know."

Shay grimaced. "How big are these 'alien circles' exactly?"

"Not too big," Daniel replied. "But bigger than you'd like, I can tell you that. The only reason James Brownstone is allowed to walk around free is that everyone's afraid of him. No one wants to be the one who finally sets him off."

"Good. It's not that I think the bastards could take him, but he's on edge, and I don't need these Fortis fuckers spinning him up. We're trying to plan a fucking wedding."

"A wedding?" Daniel looked confused.

Shay pulled out her phone. "I better give James a call to let him know the fuckers might be coming after him. So, what's the deal, right now? I know you're not going to help me out with the job, but what about right now?"

"We'll drop you off wherever you want," Daniel explained. "But after that, we need to get out of here. I'll be blunt, Shay. We probably won't see each other for a long time."

"Fair enough." Shay nodded. "Thanks for your help. Don't worry. If you can keep these bastards mostly off us, I'll get that map to the Professor, and he'll do what he needs to do with it." She scoffed. "So we're fighting other agents to get to a vimana map so we can have a weapon against the damned Nine Systems Alliance."

Daniel let out a dark chuckle. "When you say it like that, it sounds so complicated."

Daisy snickered in the back.

Shay sighed. "Yeah. Fucking complicated."

## CHAPTER FOURTEEN

Whispy radiated eagerness. *Moderate adaptation potential. Engage and kill the enemy.*

James grunted. *Don't worry about that. There'll be all sorts of killing soon. I'm gonna make sure of it. These fuckers don't understand who they just went after.*

Drones trailed after him, but they didn't have any obvious weapons.

The F-350 screamed down the side streets, James' hands tight on the wheel as he took deep breaths. He was still processing everything Shay had just told him over the phone. He'd wanted a little more action to spice up his week, but he *hadn't* wanted government assassins coming after them.

James didn't give a shit if the Fortis assholes were rogue CIA. They'd gone after Shay. It didn't matter that she had been doing a good job of taking them out and some other CIA fucker helped her. Any group who dared attacked someone he cared about was voting for its annihilation, up to and including him blowing up buildings.

James' heart thundered in his chest and he gritted his teeth, the anger thick in the air. A low growl escaped his mouth.

*You fuckers think I won't go to war with you because you've got government connections? Screw you. I'll fucking tear up anyone who threatens Shay or Alison. You're only lucky that all those assholes are already dead.*

*Sufficient power for advanced transformation available,* Whispy reported. *Engage and kill the enemy.*

*Not yet,* James sent. *Not yet. I want these fuckers to be afraid. I want them to feel it right before I send them to Hell. That's what they get for picking the wrong woman to screw with. That's what they get for not learning the fucking lesson we already taught the government with Alison a while ago.*

James reached up to his ear to turn on the new model of receiver Heather had given him. He hadn't even had a chance to use it yet, other than to test it a few weeks prior. He had already briefly talked to the hacker on the phone and relayed what Shay had told him. That was right before he spotted the drones following him and assumed Fortis was also coming at him soon.

"Your tac drone close yet, Heather?" he rumbled. "I can't do much to those things from my truck."

"Almost there. Fortunately, you're heading right toward it. Where are you going, anyway?"

"Runyon Canyon Park. I was close anyway. I was checking out a restaurant supply store when Shay called. I figure that since it's already nighttime, there will be fewer people around, so I can fuck up these Fortis assholes without others getting caught in the crossfire. They probably brought more flashy artifact weapons and shit if they're coming after me."

"Sounds good. I'll see if I can bring up some satellite or drone imagery for the area after I finish checking on you." Heather took a deep breath. "Damn. You've still got multiple drones from what I can see on the traffic cams, but they don't look like they're armed."

James grunted. "Yeah, not worried about the drones. These fuckers aren't gonna come after me yet. They'll wait until I'm somewhere a little more deserted. They might even know where I'm going and wait for their chance." He did a mirror check. "Not seeing any vehicles looking like they're following me. Got eyes on any strange helicopters or shit like that? I don't want any surprises."

"Nope, but wait. One sec." The faint clack of typing came over the line. "There are several black SUVs driving parallel to you a few blocks over. I've been checking the nearby traffic cameras just in case. It's too perfect. Tinted windows. Looks like they are going to hit you a lot harder than they hit Shay at first."

"Then they understand who they are dealing with. Good for them. It's not gonna save them." James flexed his fingers. "The fuckers are gonna make it nice and personal. Fucking terrific. I want to look them in the eye as I fucking kill them."

"I'll let you know if the situation changes," Heather replied quietly.

A few minutes passed before James slammed on the brakes. A closed gate blocked the road, and a house sat right next to the gate.

*Fuck. The gate's closed? Damn it. Need to put some distance between this house and the fight. The whole fucking point was to keep other people out of my shit.*

James glanced to his left. A fence blocked access to a steep hill. There wasn't much in the way of cover other than a few shrubs, but he'd already bonded Whispy and wasn't concerned about avoiding attacks.

He didn't bother grabbing any weapons from the back. Whispy would be enough. He wanted to kill these so-called alien hunters with an alien weapon, if only to make a point. They needed to understand who they were allowed to mess with and who they weren't.

*Engage and kill the enemy,* Whispy insisted. *Achieve maximum adaptation for primary directive.*

*Fuck that. This is personal. You'll get what you want, but that's just because you're lucky.*

*Acceptable. Engage and kill enemy.*

James snorted as he threw open the F-350's door and stepped into the chilly LA November evening air. Not worried about the temperature, he threw his coat on the seat along with his holster and knife sheath. He pulled off his t-shirt next and set it on top of his holster.

*I wonder how smart these fuckers will be. I hope they're stupid-brave. That'll be more fun when I beat their asses into the ground.*

James marched over to and hopped the nearby chain link fence before starting up the steep shrub-covered hill. The bright moonlight made it so he didn't need any eye modifications.

He frowned and narrowed his eyes as he realized something. SUVs were zooming up the road in the distance, but he didn't see the drones anywhere. There was no light buzz in the air. Everything was still and quiet, like a graveyard. There wasn't even a breeze.

"Heather, you there?" James asked.

Silence.

"Shit, Shay warned me about jamming." He frowned.

It didn't matter. She'd already done her part by letting him know they were on the way, and jamming meant the enemy had reduced their ability to use drones. He could handle the rest by himself.

James continued climbing the hill as the SUVs screeched to a halt. Men piled out of the vehicles, most holding small silver pistols and two holding blocky gray rifles James didn't recognize. He couldn't pick out much detail from a distance, and he didn't want Whispy to modify his vision right before a fight.

*You better hope that's the world's best anti-Vax gun, fuckers, or this is gonna be a very short fight. Who am I kidding? It's gonna be a short fight anyway.*

*Engage and kill the enemy,* Whispy ordered.

*Nah. They're going to engage me, and then I'll kill them.*

"I'm here, you Fortis motherfuckers," James roared, waving his arms. "You fuckers should have attacked me before you went after Shay. Then maybe you would have had a tiny chance, but now you have none. I'm ready for you, and now you're gonna die."

The new arrivals aimed their pistols at the fence and fired. Blue beams blasted from the silver weapons and sliced through the metal, but the men with the rifles didn't fire. The agents kicked the fence down and rushed onto the hill, their weapons aimed at James.

*High potential for adaptation,* Whispy declared, a mixture of curiosity and happiness accompanying his report.

James continued to wait, his fingers twitching. He didn't need Whispy's continued taunts to urge him on to battle. He'd been ready for this from the minute Shay let him know she'd been attacked after leaving the Leanan Sidhe.

*These fuckers will die, and they don't even know it yet.*

The men fanned out, crushing the shrubs under their feet as they advanced slowly up the hill.

"James Brownstone," one of the agents called. "You're in possession of illegal technology that represents a threat to the national security of the United States. You are to immediately turn over said technology and surrender to us."

"There's no fucking law against this shit." James slapped his palm over Whispy, who had sunk into the center of his chest. "You telling me there's some sort of Vax Technology Control Law or some shit? Fuck you, assholes."

"So you acknowledge you're currently using alien technology?"

"I acknowledge I'm about to fuck you up, and I'll fucking end anyone who helps you."

The men continued their advance. A porch light turned on from the house on the opposite side of the fence, and a man in a robe stepped outside.

*Shit. Stay inside.*

One of the Fortis agents turned and shot him through the chest with his silver energy pistol. The poor bastard didn't even have time to scream before he tumbled to the porch, dead.

James growled. "You fucking sonsofbitches."

*Sufficient power for advanced transformation,* Whispy reiterated.

*Do it.*

The armor spread from the amulet, the sound of the ripping pants clear in the otherwise still night. The blade extended, and James let out a low growl.

"If you are smart government assholes, then you should know you don't have a chance against me," James rumbled.

The previous speaker shook his head. "We've got a few more tools available than your common criminal, and we understand your anti-magic potential."

The advancing Fortis agents stopped but didn't fire.

"We don't need you, Brownstone," the man continued. He hadn't even bothered to turn around when his friend murdered an innocent man. "We just need the symbiont. If you claim to care about this country and this planet at all, you'll surrender it to us. It's safest with us. We can study it. Find out its weaknesses. Think about it—we could be ready if the Vax ever come to this planet."

James snorted. "You just fucking killed some poor sonofabitch for stepping onto his porch. Fuck you. I'm not giving you shit. Besides that, you fuckers went after Shay. Those guys are dead, and now you're going to die. You shouldn't be worried about the Vax coming here. You should worry about the Vax right in front of you."

Whispy's eager joy was palpable.

The agent nodded slowly. "So that's how it's going to be." He holstered his pistol and reached into his pocket, and a moment later, Alison appeared in the grass and shrubs, kneeling and blindfolded, with her hands bound behind her. Cuts and bruises covered her face.

"Alison?" James called, his heartbeat kicking into a gallop. "What the fuck?"

*Engage and kill the enemy.*

*Shut the fuck up and let me concentrate.*

"I'm scared, Dad," Alison whimpered. "I don't know what happened. They've done something. My magic doesn't work."

"Nothing like a little alien teleportation tech. Much better than portals." The Fortis agent pulled out his gun and aimed it at her head. "Your choice, Brownstone. Your symbiont or your daughter."

Rage flooded James. His vision swam, and his entire body trembled. His bellow of anger echoed around the hill. Several of the agents stepped back, the calm gone from their faces.

James took a single step forward. "Get. The. Fuck. Away. From. Her."

The agent pressed the gun to the back of Alison's head. "Uh, uh, uh, Brownstone. One more step and I introduce her brains to a direct plasma beam at point-blank range. We've neutralized her magic, so there's no shield protecting her."

Several of the other agents stepped farther back at James' loud growl.

*Power sufficient for extended advanced transformation,* Whispy reported. *Engage and kill the enemy.*

Tears rolled down Alison's cheeks. "Please, Dad. Just give them what they want. I'm so scared."

James stopped moving and narrowed his eyes.

*Big mistake, fucker.*

"Good boy, Brownstone," the Fortis agent shouted. "You of all people can't question someone using a little excess force during a job. Sometimes it's necessary for the greater good. This is just a little more important than removing a few criminals from the streets. This is about saving the planet from potential alien invaders. The way I see it, you don't have a choice. The whole planet followed your little adoption hearing. We know how important this girl is to you."

James continued staring at Alison and the gun. Even in the anger and hatred swirling through his body and mind, something was screaming for him to notice. He finally did. The Fortis agent had leaned forward, and the tip of his weapon had disappeared into the back of Alison's head.

*It's a fucking trick.*

The realization didn't kill the waves of anger radiating through his body. Whispy had always been that good at keeping that kind of thing going.

*Kill the enemy. Kill the enemy. Kill the enemy.*

*Fuck it. I was gonna do it anyway. Let's go the next step.*

The remainder of his armor appeared, along with his claws and helmet, his expanded vision coming in a moment later. The Fortis agents let out a startled gasp, except for the lead agent, who still hadn't realized his error. His face wore a smug grin, the mask of a too-confident fool.

James pointed a blade at the agent. "You made a big mistake, asshole," he growled. "You shouldn't have tried to fool me with a fake Alison. You die first, and you die painfully."

The lead agent sighed and looked down at this gun. "Oh, shit. Whatever. I'm tired of this. Use the blast pistols. We can still study the corpse."

The image of Alison disappeared, and he raised his weapon.

Blue beams lit up the night and buzzed as shot after shot after shot struck him, the beam dissipating across his armor.

*Near maximum adaptation already achieved against attack type,* Whispy reported, disappointment filtering in with the thought.

James had no idea when he'd run into plasma beams before, nor did he care. He still had a fucker to kill. With a roar, he launched himself into the air and raised his blade.

The Fortis agents continued firing, but their shots weren't doing anything more than scraping a thin layer off the armor. James brought his blade down and sliced the lead agent in half. The man's blood splattered and coated the agents near him.

As the man's body split into pieces, James growled, "Told you that you'd die first."

He charged another man and decapitated him before ripping out a man's throat with his claws. The two agents with the rifles backed away as James carved through the rest of the agents with ease. Neither had fired. Both were furiously tapping on some sort of keypads on the sides of the weapons.

*Huh. Should have had that shit ready. Why is this crap so locked down?*

One of the riflemen turned and rushed down the hill

toward the cars. The other raised his weapon, his body shaking.

*Warning: unusual resonance detected,* Whispy reported. *Caution recommended.*

*Caution? Since when the fuck are you worried about an attack? You always want new adaptations. Don't suddenly become a pussy.*

James let out a long low growl as he stalked toward the fleeing agent.

The man raised his gun and fired. James' left arm disappeared in a cloud of purple lilac-scented smoke. He was too surprised for the pain to set in before he sliced the man and weapon in half.

*Yesssssss,* Whispy sent. Then, as if realizing the situation added, *Extreme damage detected. Regeneration in progress. Adaptation in progress. Prioritizing adaptation.*

James bellowed a mix of rage and pain and pointed his blade at the line of cars. Green light formed over the blade as he sent an energy attack at the vehicles, the pain continuing to cloud his mind.

The green beam blasted from his blade-cannon and raked the street, slicing through the cars and carving a thin path through the asphalt. Several of the cars exploded, and the rest collapsed into pieces.

The fleeing agent spun, his eyes wide with terror as an extremely pissed, one-armed, fully armored Vax advanced on him.

The rifle flashed, and the top layer of James' armor turned to soft feathers and flaked off with the breeze.

*Primary adaptation achieved,* Whispy reported. *Rebalancing regeneration and adaptation.*

"No, this is impossible," the surviving Fortis agent shouted as he fired again. "Nothing's immune to this thing. That was why they stashed them around to begin with."

The space around James' armor shimmered for a second, a thin layer of gummy bears appeared and fell to the ground.

James raised his remaining arm. "There's always a defense," he snarled.

"You can't still be alive," the agent complained.

James stabbed the man through the heart and the agent coughed up blood, blinking in surprise before his head slumped forward. The bounty hunter yanked his blade out, and the dead agent pitched backward and rolled down the hill, his weapon at James' feet. A few hacks with the blade shredded the weapon.

The pain on James' side started to ebb slightly as symbiont tendrils extended to his wound to form a scaffold for a new arm.

*What the fuck was that?* James sent, his side throbbing, and his heart pounding, his anger and hatred fueling a desire to kill more enemies even though everyone in the area was dead.

*Molecular-scale rearrangement. Transformation mechanism unknown.*

*You can adapt to something without even knowing what it is?*

*Yes. Recommend external healing via supplemental means for rapid regeneration of missing limb.*

James growled and walked over to another Fortis body. He stabbed it a few more times, the blows jostling his body and increasing his pain. He marched down toward the truck. He had a few healing potions hidden inside. He had no idea how long it'd take to grow back an arm without the help of a potion.

No pity lingered in his heart for the men he'd just killed. He spared a glance for the dead man on the porch.

James' only regret was that he hadn't killed the agents before they'd gunned the man down.

*Fucking Fortis.*

## CHAPTER FIFTEEN

"I need to know that she's okay," James shouted into the phone.

"I assure you, Mr. Brownstone," Headmistress Mara Berens explained over the phone, "Alison is fine. More than fine. No one has penetrated the school's defenses, and she's safe and sound. There's not even a hint that an enemy has penetrated the school grounds in recent weeks."

*How can she be safe when Fortis is around? That might have been a trick, but going after her does make sense. They might already be on their way.*

"Why can't I get her on her phone?" James rumbled. "I tried calling, and it just keeps going to voicemail. How do you know they didn't snatch her?"

"I just used a spell to verify that she's in her room," the woman replied with a soft sigh. "I understand your concern, but we're always changing our wards," the headmistress explained. "It's one of the reasons we don't recommend students bring phones; they can fail at a moment's notice, and in some cases, they might represent a way to get through our defenses as a magical anchor. We're considering banning them, to be honest, but as I said, she's currently in her room. I can summon her to the phone if you want. The last thing we want is a worried parent, especially you."

James sighed, a little of his concern fading. Even though he knew the Alison he'd just seen was a fake, the anger and concern had lingered. He still wished there were more agents to kill.

*Fuckers didn't study me hard enough if they thought that shit was going to go down the way they hoped.*

"Nah," James offered. "If I make her come to the phone, she'll just worry. Thanks for letting me know, and sorry to bother you so late at night. Just, stuff happens in my line of work, and I saw something that got me worried about her."

"It's no problem." Headmistress Berens cleared her throat. "Let me ask you one thing, Mr. Brownstone. The trouble you're concerned about; is it magical in nature? We can handle it regardless of its nature, but the more we know about any potential threats to the school, the easier we can customize our response."

"No, the assholes I'm dealing with use technology. Advanced technology. Probably more advanced than you're used to, but there's nothing magical about it."

Mara let out a sigh of relief. "Then I can assure you that they won't get anywhere near her. Magic does have certain advantages, even over the most advanced technology. There are more than a few frustrated government agents who both envy and fear our school's defenses."

*Yeah, I bet you some of those asshole work for Fortis, too.*

"Thanks," James replied. "Like I said, sorry to bother

you. Don't tell Alison. She doesn't need to worry about something she can't fix, and I'll make sure this problem is over soon."

"It's no bother, and I'll keep this between us. I agree that stressing out Alison wouldn't do either of you any good. Is there anything else, Mr. Brownstone?"

"No, I'm good."

"Try to have a good night." With that, Mara hung up.

James grunted.

*Yeah, I was having a good night until CIA assholes came and tried to kill Shay and me. It's been the same for a long time, all the way back to the Harriken. I'm minding my own business, and those fuckers can't leave me alone. They have to come blow my arm off and get in my face.*

James shook out his new left arm. He'd lost a hand before and regenerated it, but he'd never lost a full arm. He was impressed. No pain, and it felt just like the old one. At first glance, it looked identical, but he hadn't carefully inspected any of the patterns or looked to see if the old scars were still there.

It didn't really matter. All he cared about was whether he'd be able to use it when he needed to in a fight.

Whispy had gone into quiescent mode as he continued the background regeneration work.

*Fuck. How much of me could get blown away and fixed? Does he have a backup of my brain if it gets taken out, or would it just be him calling the shots in a mindless body?*

James checked his mirrors again to be sure. No one was following him.

He was on his way to Warehouse Five to rendezvous with Shay. He'd collected the blast pistols and fragments of the rifles to store in her vault there. There was no reason to leave it around for the government, good agents or bad, to collect. Fortis had tried to kill him, so he claimed their weapons as a bonus.

"James, can you talk now?" Heather asked through his ear receiver.

He'd requested that she not talk to him for a few minutes when he'd first gotten back in his truck, even though the jamming had cleared when he destroyed the SUVs. The whole process of regenerating his limb wasn't as comfortable as he would have liked, and he didn't feel like explaining it to her.

"Yeah," James rumbled. "I'm good. What's up?"

Heather sighed. "Sorry about not being more help back there. Those bastards were using pretty powerful jamming, even optical. I couldn't even see what was happening with hacked remote drones. In some ways, what these guys did was more impressive than what Erin North pulled off."

*Humans outperforming aliens; I'm impressed. Maybe Earth* does *have a chance against the Alliance. They probably stole that shit from some other aliens, but they got it working.*

James grunted. "They've got access to some fancy-ass tech. Doesn't matter. They're all dead now. All their fancy tech didn't do shit to save them in the end. If anything, it's the reason they're dead. They pulled stuff they shouldn't have to fuck with me. Between the dead guys who went after Shay and the guys I killed, they lost a lot of men tonight."

The steering wheel creaked under his grip, the memory of the image of the beaten Alison flickering through his mind. If the Fortis agents hadn't gotten him so pissed, he might not have been able to transform into extended advanced mode and survive the super-rifle attacks, even with his basic adaptation ability.

*How angry is a true Vax Forerunner?*

"Some other CIA-looking guys showed up, and new jamming started up a few minutes after you left," Heather explained, "Peyton contacted me right before and said not to worry about it."

"I'm betting they're with that Daniel guy." James sighed. "This shit is annoying. I don't care if he's supposed to be a good guy. He's still a government spy. He should have kept these assholes away from us. I don't ask other people to clean up my messes, and I don't like having to clean up theirs."

"Peyton and I are continuing to coordinate," Heather explained. "We're both on high alert and watching the systems. I'm assuming these guys will come at you again in different ways. Now that we know who is behind everything, we can make sure they don't win on the cyber front. If we can deal with an alien hacker, we can handle humans, no matter what fancy tech they are using."

James nodded. "Thanks. You two watch our asses online. Shay and I will handle the rest."

Shay ran her fingers over James' bicep, her eyebrows raised. "It feels the same. I should know, I touch it enough. You regenerated a whole new limb in a few minutes? Damn! That's impressive, even for extended advanced mode. You're getting more ridiculous with each passing month."

James lowered his arm and shrugged. "I was pretty pissed off, and I still needed the healing potion to do it that quickly. Who knows how long it would have taken otherwise? And I still had to win the fight. If the guy had been able to shoot straight, I might be dead."

"You're still alive, and they're all dead. I wouldn't underestimate how useful this will be." Shay laughed. "And the point is, it would have still grow back. Say it took a couple of days; that wouldn't be the end of the world, and it's still a step up. It takes major healing magic to regenerate limbs." She nodded at the pile of rifle parts. "I'm guessing Daniel's people will eventually ask for all that crap back. I have no idea if they know about the warehouses. I want to say no, but I can't be sure."

"I don't give a shit if they want them back. Finders-fucking-keepers, especially when the finding involves some asshole vaporizing my arm into smelly purple smoke." James growled. "If they wanted to get their hands on this shit, they should have done a better job of keeping Fortis off our asses to begin with."

Shay folded her arms over her chest and nodded. "If we do the Professor's vimana job, this might not be the end of it. Daniel and his friends are going to do what they can, but as tonight proved, they can't always protect us. I'm sure we'll run into more of these guys."

James picked up a piece of the rifle barrel. "We don't need protection. After tonight's bullshit, there's no fucking way I'm walking away. Fuck Fortis with their weird-ass guns and fake Alisons." He tossed the piece back on the table. "But I don't trust Daniel either. He's another government spy running around trying to hide shit from people, and I don't like that he knows everything about you now. He might try to use that shit against you."

"True," Shay replied, "but I don't care. Plenty of people know the truth, including Maria. Even if I did have the ambush under control, it was helpful to have him there, and more to the point, we now know a lot about him, too. And this isn't the first time he's helped me." She shrugged. "Not saying I trust him, just he doesn't seem like the kind of person who will murder some man on his porch. And now that you've adapted to some of the fancier alien tech, who knows if they even have a way to stop you?"

James grunted. "You're saying they won't fuck with you because they're afraid of me?"

"If they're not stupid, they won't, but there are a lot of stupid people in the world, so we can't be sure." Shay picked up one of the blast pistols. "Daniel had one of these too, but I don't think I want to use anything I don't know how to easily recharge. It doesn't hurt to have a few of them in the vault, though. You never know when it might come in handy to kill an alien or two."

James slammed his fist on the table, and the fragments bounced. "Not letting those fuckers get that map. I'd do it for free after that bullshit. I hope they come after us so I can kill more of them. Maybe they will learn the fucking lesson I tried to teach the Harriken."

Shay nodded. "Looks like we're taking a trip to the Indian Ocean, then."

"You gonna bring Lily?" James uncurled his fist. "Not

saying you shouldn't, but this is more serious than usual, and it's got a lot of baggage."

Shay shook her head. "It's not that she can't handle herself in danger—she's more than proven that at this point—but you're right. This government conspiracy crap is more trouble than she needs when her life has just started to become stable. We'll help the Professor get his flying castle, and if we get lucky, we'll take out a few murderous assholes in the process."

CHAPTER SIXTEEN

S *hit. This is just another reason to be pissed at Fortis.*
The motorized skiff hit another stiff wave, and
James' stomach churned. As much as he hated planes, he'd
forgotten there was one thing he hated even worse: boats.
The sun beat down on him as their tiny boat took them
from the east coast of Tanzania to their target, a small
island long since abandoned by most of civilization. The
island held the ruins of a fallen sultanate.

James peered at the white-capped waves around them
and grunted.

*Fucking ocean. Can't even drink the water. How do you have
all that water and you can't drink it? That's the greatest bullshit
in the world.*

*Cool monsters to fight in the ocean, though, I'll give it that. I
can fight a shark, but it would be hard to fight a dragon without
having wings.*

Another wave attacked James' stomach, and he
wondered if a Vax invasion of Earth would fail because of
all the water.

Their boat driver gave James' a thumbs-up. "I can see the island now, boss." His accent colored the words and somehow made them easier for James to understand despite the loud roar of the engine. The man gave him a toothy grin but kept his hands on the wheel. "If you need to throw up, try and do it into the ocean. The fish could use it, and it saves me the trouble of cleaning the boat." When he smiled, the creases in his weathered dark skin looked even more pronounced.

James grunted and leaned forward. It was a good thing he hadn't eaten much after they'd arrived in Dar es Salaam. The flight had killed his appetite, and Shay had wanted to leave right away, so they hadn't stopped anywhere. She'd eaten a few meal bars on the way, and he figured he'd survive until later.

*If God had wanted us to fly, he would have given us wings. If he wanted us to swim, he would have given us gills.*

James nodded, satisfied with his impeccable logic.

Shay sat next to James, her face its normal color. She showed no signs of seasickness. She leaned over to whisper, "Just bond Whispy. You look like you're turning into one of those frog guys from Russia."

James turned toward her. "Whispy? How could he help?"

"If he can do shit like change your eyes, I'm sure he can do something about your little problem. We've paid this guy decent money to take us to a dangerous island, and we have weapons with us, so he'll just assume it's a magical artifact, even if he knows what's going on."

James reached under his shirt and pulled the spacer off.

The pain was a welcome distraction from the relentless churning in his stomach.

*Initiation,* Whispy sent.

*Do something about this fucking seasickness,* James commanded.

*Adjusting inner ear fluid balance. Mild defensive reduction required.*

*It's fine. Shift shit back once we're on the island.*

It was good to know about potential issues if he ever had to have a major fight on a ship in the future.

A sharp piercing pain shot through his ears for a brief second, then receded.

James blinked several times as his stomach settled. "Huh, that shit worked. Good call."

Shay nodded at the driver. "He didn't notice," she whispered.

"Ten or fifteen more minutes," the driver offered. He muttered something in Swahili before switching back to English. "I'm glad to take your money, but let me tell you what I tell all the treasure hunters. Those ruins have been empty for hundreds of years. No refunds, though, boss." He shook his head. "The rebels use the place too. They don't much like treasure hunters."

Shay chuckled. "We know. You already told us."

"Maybe you don't understand, though. These aren't like in movies. They won't show respect for your bravery. They'll take you and use you as hostages if they don't kill you, or worse. Ruthless killers, the rebels, even if they're all fools."

"Fools?"

"The war," the boat driver explained, gesturing with one

hand. "Men pledging themselves to a *mchawi* king." He shook his head. "*Mchawi* are everywhere now. He's not special. They have others in the rebel army, so why follow him?" He frowned.

"What's a *mchawi?*" James asked.

"A wizard," Shay explained.

The other man furrowed his brow and mimicked flourishing a wand with his hand. "Wizard. Yes. Sorcerer." He looked at them both and pointed to the pendant around Shay's neck. "It's magic, yes?"

Shay nodded. "Among other things."

The driver nodded. "Maybe you'll survive, then. I don't hate the rebels, but I don't mind if they die either."

The island grew closer. They were heading straight toward a stretch of open beach that quickly gave way to a dense forest. There was no sign of rebel forces, magical or otherwise.

James grinned. "Yeah, I'm not afraid of a few wizards. Do you recognize me?"

The man stared at him for a few seconds before turning his head forward. "Are you son of the man who was in the movie about the runaway train? You were in the one about the man who is a runaway dragon, right? *Two Wings of Terror?*"

Shay laughed.

James chuckled. "Nah. Not an actor." He shrugged, not insulted that the man didn't recognize him. Sometimes having a rep made things easier, but here it wasn't necessary. "Just think of me as the hired muscle."

The beach grew larger as they moved closer. A few

seagulls circled overhead. There was still no sign of any rebels.

The driver slowed the boat. "Everything is as I told the woman. You call me on the satellite phone and I'll come to get you, but it will take two hours. I will wait for two days. If you don't call me by then, I will assume you're dead and offer a prayer for your souls."

Shay checked her tactical vest and grabbed her backpack. "Understood."

"If rebels are on the beach when I come, I won't pick you up. They leave me alone, but I don't interfere with their business either."

James grunted. "Unless they want fewer rebels, they'll leave us the fuck alone."

"That's the spirit, boss." The driver pulled the throttle back even more and slowed the boat to a crawl toward the beach. "Your boots waterproof?"

Shay nodded. "Yeah." She slipped her backpack on and nodded to James.

He also put on his backpack and checked all the straps on his tactical vest.

The driver killed the engine, letting the skiff drift forward until it stopped in the shallow water.

Shay hopped out of the boat, the water splashing around her boots. James followed. A few steps took both of them into the wet sand of the rocky beach.

The driver waved and put the boat in reverse. "Don't die. I need the other half of your money."

Shay smirked. "We'll keep that in mind."

James looked around the dense trees. "You said there are no monsters on the island?"

Shay shook her head. "I said I hadn't heard anything about monsters on the island. It's like our friend on the boat said. I've mostly heard that rebels occasionally use the island. If there were a bunch of monsters on it, I doubt they would hang out there, even if they have wizards with them."

They continued toward the tree line.

James looked over his shoulder at the retreating boat. "Why hasn't anyone found the map, then?"

"Because they didn't know it was here. Even if they did, they didn't have the activation incantations that Smite-Williams passed along to me to reveal the stupid thing." Shay made a pained face. "Or if they did, they didn't have the patience to go through dozens of them. Love how he didn't mention that part until we were just about to leave."

James chuckled. "Saying shit's less annoying than fighting." Pain shot through his ears, and he grimaced.

"What's wrong?" Shay looked concerned.

James held up a hand. "It's fine." The pain faded. "Just Whispy readjusting my ears to land mode."

"Huh. That makes sense."

*Inner ear fluid balance readjusting for maximum land efficiency,* Whispy reported.

Shay knelt and pulled her backpack off. She reached inside and removed a metal box. She flipped the lid and pulled out two folded-up microdrones. After unfolding the drones, she wiped off their solar cells and set them on the ground.

James slipped in his ear receiver, and Shay did as well. She took a moment to link the receivers with her satellite phone.

"Are you there, Peyton?" Shay asked.

Peyton's loud, long yawn came through the receiver. "It's past my bedtime. I should get overtime."

They'd decided that Peyton would take first support watch, and Heather would sleep and take over by the time it hit the evening local time, which would be morning for her and Peyton. Time zones were the eternal bane of international jobs.

A whine came from the two drones, and they rose.

"These aren't the best, but nice for a quick island hop," Peyton explained.

"I didn't want to haul more than we could easily carry with us," Shay explained. "Especially since this was a quick island hop, and things are unstable because of the war. It's also why I didn't bring the *tachi*. It might stand out a bit."

"You just brought Brownstone," Peyton observed.

"True, but he just looks like any other thug mercenary around here.'

James chuckled. "'Any other thug mercenary?'"

"Well, a handsome one." Shay winked.

Peyton cleared his throat. "If you could stop flirting for a second, I've got some information for you. According to the satellite density scans, you should just head northeast from your current position. Walking a few miles inland should bring you to the ruins, and it looks like most of the old stone road is still there, so it won't be a painful walk."

Shay pulled out her phone and brought up the compass app before nodding. "Easy enough." She grabbed her backpack and put it back over her shoulders. "If we're lucky, we won't even run into any rebels."

Thirty minutes later, they were walking along the remnants of a stone road in the center of the forest. The high trees surrounding them protected them from the worst of the midday sun, but their sparse placement allowed plenty of the blue sky to peep through.

"Trouble," Peyton reported.

James grunted and slowed his pace. "Trouble?"

Shay frowned and pulled out her 9mm. "Care to elaborate?"

"I've tagged ten guys coming your way, nine with rifles and one with some sort of gold-tipped wooden staff. They are creeping along slowly. I think they were hoping for an ambush. Hard for me to make out a lot of details with the drones from a distance, but if I get any closer, they'll probably take it out. Wait."

Shay furrowed her brow. "What's wrong?"

Thunder echoed through the forest.

"What the hell was that?" James asked.

Peyton groaned. "Yeah, the staff is the guy's wand. He just took out both the drones with some sort of lightning spell."

Shay chuckled. "So now they know they won't be able to ambush us. They'll probably rush us instead."

"Good," James replied. "It helps to get shit over with."

*Minimum adaptation potential,* Whispy complained. *Kill enemies and proceed to stronger enemies for maximum adaptation potential.*

Several men shouted in the distance. Shay activated her

defensive artifacts but didn't raise her gun. James folded his arms over his chest and waited.

Men in green and yellow camouflage uniforms emerged from the trees, their AKs pointed at James and Shay. Their wizard brought up the rear with his gold-topped dark wood staff. They sprinted toward the couple and spread out around them in a half-circle, all shouting.

They fell silent as the wizard stepped forward and grinned at James. "Too big to be a tourist." His gaze cut to Shay's gun. "And too well-armed for tourists." He gestured at Shay. "And the magical silver around your skin. Some sort of artifact? More tomb raiders who have come to pick the carcass of the Sultanate clean? You're hundreds of years too late, but your kind keeps coming."

"I'm not going to deny I'm a tomb raider, but what I'm looking for isn't valuable to you," Shay replied. "You probably won't believe this, but me getting what I'm looking for will actually benefit you, along with a lot of other people on Earth in the long run. So, why don't you guys all turn around and leave us alone? There doesn't have to be trouble."

He chuckled and said something to his men in a mixture of Arabic and Swahili. They all laughed.

"Put down your weapons, tomb raider," the wizard ordered. "I'm sure there's someone back in Australia who is willing to pay for you."

James grunted. "Australia? We're Americans."

The wizard shrugged. "All your accents sound the same to me."

"How the fuck does an American accent sound the same as an Australian accent?"

Shay eyed James. "Is this really the conversation we need to be having right now?"

*Kill the enemy,* Whispy recommended.

*I'm thinking about it.*

James cracked his knuckles and stepped forward. "I'm James Brownstone. I don't give a shit about your rebellion; I'm just here to help her get something. We don't have time to drag your ass somewhere for a bounty, so you can back the fuck off, or you can die."

The wizard looked him up and down. "James Brown-stone?" He turned to his men and shrugged. "James Brownstone?"

They all shrugged back.

Shay snickered. "You need better PR in East Africa, apparently."

James grunted. It didn't matter if they didn't know who he was. A reputation was just a record of achievements, and he could start a new record there with these men.

He stepped toward the wizard. The men all shouted and pointed their guns at his chest.

"Better shoot me," James rumbled. "Or better yet, get the fuck out of my way, because if you don't, I'm gonna force you the fuck out of my way."

The wizard snorted. "Kill him."

The men fired in near perfect synchronicity, a crack volley of high-powered bullets that would have shredded most men. The bullets ripped through his overshirt and t-shirt before bouncing off his hardened skin.

*Maximum adaptation achieved against attack type,* Whispy observed.

James shrugged. "That all you got? Fuck, at this rate, there's no way you'll win your little rebellion."

The wizard pointed at James' head. "Shoot him there, fools."

Nine bullets struck his head but left only a few scratches.

The men took a few steps back, fear on their faces.

The wizard muttered something under his breath before pointing his staff at James' chest. Sparks danced around the tip for a few seconds before a white bolt crackled from the staff and slammed into James' chest.

The acrid scent of his charred clothing filled the air. The attack blew a hole through his shirt and undershirt and singed his tactical vest, but it'd only left him with a slight sting and some redness. The damage to his clothes revealed the amulet beneath.

*Maximum adaptation achieved against attack type*, Whispy observed.

The wizard's eyes widened as he also stepped back. "You have a powerful artifact."

James nodded. "You want to keep this shit up or should I just kill you now? We don't have time for too much fun."

The wizard sprinted for the trees, and the other men fell in behind him.

Shay laughed and holstered her gun. "Now that wasn't very fair."

James' eyes flicked down for a moment as he took in his chest. With the amulet half-embedded and the shape of the many tendrils visible beneath his skin, it must have looked like the amulet was trying to consume him. In a way, that was true.

"They were the dumbasses who attacked us without knowing if they could win," James muttered. "Not my fault they didn't know who they were fucking with. At least they were smart enough to run away."

Shay shook her head. "No, that's not what I'm getting at."

"What then?"

"They shot you with bullets and a spell, and I didn't get a chance to threaten them before they ran."

"That important?" James asked.

"No. Just fun. You're not the only one who likes to screw with people's heads." Shay pointed into the forest. "We should get going." They had walked only a few yards when she spoke next. "Peyton, you still there?"

"Yes, I'm still here," the hacker responded.

"I'll get another microdrone up and running, but it's the last one," Shay explained. "You'll still need to watch our asses once we find the place in case those assholes decide to come back with something more impressive, like a tank."

"Okay," Peyton responded, half-yawning. "I'll double-check all your flight stuff out of the country and go get something with caffeine."

"Thanks."

CHAPTER SEVENTEEN

No one else bothered Shay and James during the rest of their hike through the forest. The ruins consisted of piles of old stones and a few half-standing walls. Something impressive might have once stood on the island, but nature, or perhaps other tomb raiders past and present, had long since stripped it down to its current sad state. The remnants of the stone road leading to the ruins were more impressive than anything at the site.

Shay pulled her AR goggles out of her backpack and slipped them on. She set them to thermal mode, and soon found a noticeable thermal differential in a round shape in the ground and walked to the shrub-covered dirt. "I think this is going to get annoying, or at least as annoying as a normal archaeological dig, but it's as good a time as any to get used to it."

James headed toward her. "Why? What's wrong?"

Shay pulled a collapsible shovel off the side of her backpack and expanded it. "Because I'm pretty sure this is the entrance to the tunnel. Underground, anyway. According to the Professor's briefing information, I should be able to put my hand on the entrance and say the opening incantation and get inside, but I've got to be able to touch it directly for that to work."

"That doesn't sound so bad." James stared at the ground.

"Sure, but it means we've got to dig it up. From what I can tell with my goggles, it's a few feet down and at an angle. Any explosives might collapse the tunnel, so it's time for some good old-fashioned digging. It's interesting, though." Shay scratched her eyelid. "I looked over satellite imagery in different bands for this area, and so did Peyton. According to all those images, there's nothing buried on this island."

"Cover-up?" James suggested.

"Maybe, or possibly just a decent spell. Even if the people who set it up didn't know about satellites, it might have been some sort of general defense to protect it from tracking from far away." Shay crouched and picked at the dirt. "One thing doing this job has taught me is never to underestimate the ancients."

"It doesn't matter. We're here now." James grunted and held his hand out. "Give me the shovel. I'll get this shit finished as soon as possible."

Shay passed the shovel to him. "I knew I should have brought two shovels."

---

The minutes went by as James flung dirt and rock over his shoulder with surprising speed. His efforts had revealed most of the dark circular stone door, but Shay was looking for a particular combination of glyphs to touch before she used the entrance incantation. She could detect mild heat emanating from the door with her goggles, but there was nothing to pinpoint the location of the activation glyphs.

*This is what I'll be doing for the university, too—going around telling other people to dig things up. I'll be looking for lost secrets with fewer killings. It might be less adrenaline-filled, but still interesting in its own non-lethal way.*

Then again, the very nature of modern archaeology post-opening of the gates added more inherent danger. Many archaeological digs required at least some precautions in case they encountered a bizarre magical trap or threat. If Shay could provide that for herself with the cover that she'd been trained by James Brownstone, people might not even find it odd.

"Last thing I thought I was gonna do today was dig," James commented. "Kind of relaxing, even if Whispy bitches every once in a while about finding someone to kill."

Shay smirked. "If you want to quit the bounty-hunting game, you would make a good gravedigger."

"Probably. I've sure sent enough people to their graves." James' muscles glistened with the exertion. Although he exercised a lot at home, it'd been a while since he'd done basic physical labor that didn't involve kicking someone's ass or hauling around meat, especially in a tropical climate.

"We still clear, Peyton?" Shay asked. "No tanks or helicopters or wizards riding dragons?"

"I'm still doing a wide perimeter with the drone, but the satellite info from a few minutes ago showed the rebels on their way to a boat on the opposite side of the island." Peyton whistled. "You scared them off their own hideout. Nice. You didn't even have to kill any of them."

"I'm less worried about those assholes than I am Fortis agents," Shay replied, staring at James' left arm for a moment. Even if he'd regenerated it, that didn't change the fact that they'd destroyed it, which meant there was a possibility they could hurt him again. He was tough, but he wasn't invulnerable.

James continued to shovel, oblivious to Shay's eyes and concern.

"I've hacked into the systems at Julius Nyerere in Dar es Salaam," Peyton explained.

"The airport? Why did you do that?" Shay frowned.

"So I could also get access to their radar," Peyton explained. "You're close enough to the mainland that I might be able to use those as early warning systems if something suspicious and high-speed heads your way. Also doing my best to keep you in sight with different satellites. The drone might not be the most effective, but I've got your back. The only thing is, I'm going to lose you once you go underground."

"We'll be fine underground," Shay replied. "There might be some zombies or monsters or giant spiders or whatever down there, but we're expecting that. I just don't want to be surprised by any assholes with alien ray guns."

James grunted as he launched another shovelful of dirt away from the hole. He'd now completely revealed the massive circular door leading into the tunnels beneath them. He jammed the shovel blade into the ground and wiped the sweat off his brow.

"Not a bad hole. And Whispy's already immune to their weird-ass gun," he explained. "Not worried about it anymore. I think they're out of tricks."

"But they might have *another* weird-ass gun," Shay replied.

James shrugged. "Sounds fun."

Shay sighed and shook her head. "Just watch our asses, okay, Peyton?"

"Will do."

James nodded to the door. "Now that I've done all the hard work, you gonna come and open it and take all the credit?"

Shay grinned and headed toward the door, looking it over until she found the symbols she sought in the upper-right. "Something like that." She placed her hand on the symbols and rattled off the Arabic phrase she'd memorized from the briefing materials. "Hope this works."

Nothing happened.

"Shit. Maybe we *will* have to blow—"

With a loud crunch, the doorway slid away, revealing a dark tunnel gently sloping into the ground.

Shay shrugged. "Or not." She lowered her goggles and changed them to normal optics before activating her headlamp. "Let's go find ourselves a map artifact."

James fished a headlamp out of his backpack. "I'll take point. Might get lucky and get exposed to some new attack types." He stepped inside without waiting for confirmation.

Shay followed him with a frown. "We're not sure if you can survive something like being decapitated, so you might want to still be careful."

"That's funny, coming from you."

"What's that supposed to mean?"

James grinned. "You've never seemed all that worried any of the times you were shooting me or trying to blow me up in a warehouse."

"That was a carefully controlled training environment," Shay insisted. "Even if it *was* fun."

"See?" James grunted and stepped through the doorway. "I'll be fine. It's fucking rare that I run into something totally new anymore."

They proceeded deeper into the tunnels, the sunlight from the surface slowly giving way to dusty darkness. Their headlamps kept the shadows at bay, and the temperature went down until it was chilly but not cold. The tunnel leveled out into an angled two-way inter-section.

"See?" James commented. "No traps so far."

Shay switched her AR goggles to thermal mode and looked around, but everything in the tunnel system was the same cool background temperature. The only thermal differentials in the entire area were from James and her.

"I've got nothing. Peyton, you there?"

He didn't respond.

"Not surprising," James commented. "We don't even have a decent line of sight on the entrance anymore."

Shay switched off the thermal mode of her goggles and nodded. "Let's just do this the hard way. We'll explore one path, and backtrack if we find nothing. As long as the place doesn't collapse on top of us, we should be okay."

James nodded and continued down one of the forks.

Several minutes had passed when a blade sprang from

the wall and crashed into his chest. The loud clang echoed in the hallway.

James grunted and looked down at the bent, rusty blade. "That's annoying."

"You okay?" Shay asked.

James nodded. "Yeah. Fucked up my tac vest a little, but it didn't cut me."

"We might want to be a little bit more careful."

"Maybe. If this is the best shit they've got, I'm not worried." With a dismissive snort, James continued forward.

Shay sighed and hurried after him.

<hr>

Two more blade traps and one fireball trap later, they'd returned to the initial fork in the road. James was still unharmed, but Shay's level of concern was building.

*If they had the vimana map here back in the day, that would suggest they understood what it was, which means they had access to decent magic. Those shitty traps James has tripped so far can't be the limit.*

*But maybe they've just run out of power over the centuries. Has anyone even been in these tunnels in a few hundred years? That still doesn't explain how they were able to hide the tunnels from other scans, though.*

Their trip down the other path, including several meandering turns, brought them to a dead end. A stone statue of a man in elaborate armor holding a wand stood at the end of the hallway.

"Well, this is interesting," Shay observed. "That armor

isn't what you'd expect from the Sultanate." She pointed at the carved stone wand. "And it's ballsy to display the wand openly like that."

James looked around. "You think it means something?"

"Yeah. Let's see." Shay tapped the side of her goggles to cycle back to thermal mode and looked around, detecting a hint of heat from the wall behind the statue. She pointed. "I think we might have a secret passage behind the statue."

"How do we get to it?" James looked back and forth.

Shay tapped the side of her goggles. A small window appeared in the upper-left of her field of vision. "By trying every incantation the Professor gave me. Glad I practiced my pronunciation."

———

Twenty phrases later, the top of the wand lit up and the tunnel shook.

Shay grinned. "Looks like we're in business."

James looked back and forth down the tunnel. "Or you activated the self-destruct."

"At least we'll die together." Shay tapped her foot and waited.

The grinding of stone on stone filled the chamber, and the back wall slid open. Bright blue light blinded them both, and they stumbled back.

Shay's eyes adjusted after a few seconds. A series of pulsating energy fields lined the newly revealed hidden passage. A twisting beam extended from the center of each field to the back of the chamber and a ring of crystals on the floor, an emitter of some sort. It lay right in front of an entrance to a smaller chamber.

She knelt and picked up a stray rock and tossed it at the first field, which crackled and vaporized the rock.

"That's annoying," Shay muttered. She pulled her gun and aimed at the emitter. She fired off a few rounds, but the first field destroyed them. She ejected the magazine and loaded anti-magic rounds before shooting at the emitter again. The bullet made it through several fields, but it didn't make it to the emitter before being destroyed. "That's expensive and annoying."

James grunted. "Just let me walk through, then."

"Woah." Shay shook her head. "Wait one second. Those fields are vaporizing lead on contact. We don't know if it's heat or at the atomic level or what."

James looked unimpressed. "I'll be fine."

Shay pulled out a small crystal and tossed it to him. "At least use that."

"What's this?"

"An artifact. Helps purify water. Just drain it for the magic, so you can at least have better armor coverage." Shay held up a hand. "I know, I know. He's changed you so much that you're tougher without him, but the reality is, you have that armor for a reason. Use it."

James nodded. "Fine." After removing his tactical vest and holster and handing them to Shay, he placed the crystal against his amulet, and a moment later, the silver-green metallic tendrils shot from his amulet to cover most of his body in bioarmor, although he didn't extend a blade. His helmet appeared. "Happy?"

"Satisfied," Shay responded. "Ease into it. Just try a hand

first. If the field fries it off, we can regenerate it with a potion. Wait a second, is that extended advanced mode?"

James shook his head. "I've got the helmet because I asked Whispy for it in my head, but from what he's telling me, it's not as good. He's right. I don't have the wide range of vision I normally do. He also says I don't have enough power for energy blasts or jumps."

Shay nodded. "The helmet's what's important anyway. Maximum coverage. I'd prefer you not die after all the time I've put in on wedding planning."

"Yeah. It'd be annoying when I went through all the trouble to set up the perfect proposal." James grunted and stepped toward the field with a curious look on his face. He reached out with an armored hand and touched it, then grunted and stumbled back when his fingers disappeared with a sizzle.

He shook out his hand, his face tight with pain. "Shit. Didn't expect that." His face twitched as he grabbed a healing potion from a belt pouch with his good hand and downed it.

Shay stared, refusing to blink as she watched the regeneration unfold. Tendrils extended first from the armor, and then bone formed around them, followed by muscles and then the skin. Once the fingers were back, new armor coated them.

"Imagine what five Vax like you could do," she murmured in awe.

James looked at her with a slight frown on his face. "I do all the time, which is why I need to get stronger." He lifted his newly regenerated fingers. "And this is one of the reasons I need to take risks. If they ever do come, it might come down to something I'm adapted to that they're not." He headed toward the field again and stuck his hand in it. The armor sizzled on contact but didn't vaporize. Gritting his teeth, the bounty hunter stepped through. He now stood in an empty space between two of the fields. "Going to give Whispy a moment to continue adapting. He's having a great time."

"I'm sure he is. Just remember who's in charge."

James hurried through the fields until he got to the end. His armor was sizzling and charred, but he remained in one piece. He brought back his fist and slammed it into the crystal emitter, cracking it. Several of the energy fields disappeared. A few more punches knocked large chunks off the emitter, and the rest of the fields vanished.

After a quick check with her AR goggles in several modes to assure the fields were gone, Shay jogged down to the end of the hallway to join James. His armor was already regenerating from the damage.

"I hope Whispy had fun," Shay commented. "That shit worried me."

"You never know when an adaptation would be useful." James shrugged, the gesture almost comical given the alien armor coating his body.

He pointed past the broken emitter to the interior chamber. A series of glyphs and Arabic writing covered the back wall.

Shay took a deep breath. "Time to go through my list of phrases again. Should I start from the front or the back?"

"Don't know."

Shay sighed and picked one at random she hadn't said before. In a loud, clear voice, she shouted it.

A small glass sphere winked into existence and dropped toward the floor. She jumped forward and grabbed it before it smashed against the waiting stone.

"That could have been…annoying," Shay commented with a laugh. "Sometimes it's nice to be lucky."

CHAPTER EIGHTEEN

James had reverted from advanced mode by the time they hit the exit, but they'd recovered the map, and they hadn't run into anything worse than a few more blade traps. It'd been one of the smoother tomb raids Shay'd had in a while, but being able to change symbiont modes on demand wasn't a tool they'd had access to before.

"…you…hear…?" said a voice over a static-filled line as Shay and James closed on the entrance to the tunnels.

"We can hear you, Peyton," Shay responded.

"…trouble…"

"What?" Shay's heart rate sped up.

Shay and James jogged up the sloping tunnel.

"There's trouble," Peyton explained as they cleared the tunnel, and their comm link stabilized. "I've been trying to get you for a while now. Maybe we should have set up repeaters or something."

"What trouble?" Shay asked.

"You've got a large transport plane on the way," Peyton

replied. "It's flying damned low, and it doesn't have any active transponder, so they're trying to keep out of sight. There's no way they aren't there for you."

James snorted. "There's nowhere to land on this island, let alone land a big-ass plane."

"Maybe they don't plan on landing," Peyton countered. "Maybe they just plan on shoving a huge bomb out of the back. ETA is a couple of minutes. I might be able to get the drone close since they're flying so low."

Shay looked at James. "Maybe we should break for the water just in case?"

They hurried through the trees, the hum of the approaching aircraft now audible and growing louder with each second. They were still in the trees when the plane passed directly overhead.

Shay looked up, expecting a bomb or something equally annoying, maybe a bunch of zombies in parachutes, but nothing came.

*This isn't over, so what's their game?*

James and Shay slowed but continued toward the beach.

"What's the situation, Peyton?" Shay asked.

"They're circling the island, and…opening the cargo door. Trying to get a good angle to see what's inside."

James grunted. "Big bomb it is."

Shay looked up at the plane as it flew back into their line of sight above the sparse canopy. "I don't think so."

"Why?"

Shay patted her backpack. "Because if it's Fortis, they want the vimana as much as we do, and blowing us and the map to hell won't accomplish that."

"Then why are they opening the cargo door?" James looked up. "They're letting something out."

Peyton cleared his throat. "I can answer that. From what I can see on the drone, they're about to drop a bunch of guys in exoskeletons and heavy weapons onto the island. They've got integrated anti-magic deflectors, too."

"Good." James let out a low growl. "I'd prefer a straight-up fight to all that trap shit."

"Hrmm," Peyton murmured. "This thing is a fancy turboprop."

Shay snorted. "Don't really give a shit about appreciating the enemy gear at the moment."

"No, what I'm getting at is, I think if I time it right, I can jam the drone into one of the engines. It might not crash the plane, but they'll probably at least back off."

"Do it!" Shay shouted.

"Sure thing," Peyton replied. Shay could almost hear his grin over the line.

A few seconds later, a loud pop sounded. Smoke poured from one of the engines on the plane, and it leveled out and turned toward the mainland. Several gray forms fell from the back, parasails deploying. As the new arrivals continued to drop, it grew obvious they were going to land near the beach where James and Shay had come ashore.

"Sh…I'm…think…jamming," Peyton's voice managed to get through.

Static filled the line, burying him entirely.

"Remind me to give him a proper thanks later," Shay commented. "He can be pretty useful at times."

"Is that what you say about me when I'm not around?" James asked.

Shay winked. "You bet it is."

The loud roar of a railgun sent the birds flying away from the trees. A round exploded in a nearby trunk, launching a cloud of wooden shards and dust into the air. Rifle fire from other men joined the railguns.

A bullet passed through her shields, slowed but not stopped, and skimmed her shoulder.

Shay hissed in pain but didn't stop her erratic movements among the trees. "Shit. Anti-magic rounds."

James looked her way, frowning deeply. "You okay?"

"Just a scratch, but I'm going to have to play this smart. I don't have a vest as backup. I need magical armor, not just shields." Shay forced a grin.

Another few railgun rounds blew through another tree. With a creak, the remains of the trunk snapped under the weight of the rest of the tree, bringing the entire thing down in a shower of dirt, sand, and wood.

"We've got to at least make them earn it." Shay raised her own gun, anti-magic bullets already loaded, and fired off a few rounds.

James slapped in an anti-magic magazine and joined her.

One of the parasailing men took a round between the eyes, and his head lolled forward. Fortune allowed one of Shay's 9mm rounds to sever one of the lines from the harness to another man's parasail. The other line tore a moment later, and the man plummeted toward the ground, screaming.

Shay and James reached the beach and ducked behind the tree trunks. The surviving enemies, ten in all, released their parasails several yards above the sand, their exoskeletons landing with mighty thuds.

The enemy fired James' and Shay's way, keeping them pinned.

James growled. "I'll just go out and take their fire."

Shay fired off a few rounds before slapping in another anti-magic magazine. She only had a few. "They might be able to crack your skull or something if you're not at least in advanced. How are we doing on pissing off James Brownstone?"

"I'm more annoyed than pissed." James gave her an apologetic shrug.

*We're the only couple who could get jumped by men in exoskeletons and consider it a mild annoyance.*

"It's good to be in control." Shay grabbed another crystal out of her pocket. "I've got one more little battery artifact." She tossed it to him, staying behind a tree trunk.

A railgun round struck the sand nearby, blasting the coarse substance all over them.

"Shit," Shay muttered. "It's going to be annoying to travel with that up my ass. They don't seem to have any super-guns, so if you can close on them, this should be easy-kill time."

James placed the crystal against his chest as he once again activated advanced mode. This time it was more traditional, lacking a helmet but having a blade.

"I'll lay down some cover fi—" Shay began, her gun up and her back to the tree.

An explosion blinded Shay and knocked her backward. The tree she'd been using as cover collapsed to the ground with a loud crash. She rolled through the undergrowth groaning and shaking her head. She was a little singed, but her defensive artifacts had kept her from serious harm.

"I'm okay," she muttered, shaking her head.

James' answer was a bone-rattling roar.

Shay snapped her head up and looked at him. He'd shifted into extended advanced mode and now stood there as the men pelted him with bullets and railgun rounds. The latter forced him back a few steps and dented his armor, but it wasn't annihilating him like it was the trees.

*Should I make it clear I'm okay? That must have been what set him off...*

James bent his knees and leapt into the air, his armored form hurtling toward the enemy.

With the enemy focused on shooting the approaching Vax, Shay had a chance to see the weapon that had been used against her: a hexagonal copper tube covered with intricate patterns. It spat a green-red ball of flame at James and enveloped him in a massive explosion.

*What the hell is that?* Shay thought. *The Roman Candle of Infinite Death or some shit?*

James dropped through it, showing only minor scratches and charring on his armor. He landed behind one of the railgun troops and stabbed through the back of the armored exoskeleton into the man's chest. He lifted the body, using it as a shield as he grabbed the trigger of the gun and fired a round at point-blank range into another man with a railgun.

*He's not doing this mindlessly. He might have been pissed enough to be charged up, but he's still being very strategic.*

Shay shook her head and looked around for her gun,

which she'd lost in the explosion. No reason to let James have all the fun.

He tossed the now-bullet-riddled body and exoskeleton to the ground as he rounded on the man with the Roman Candle of Infinite Death.

One of the enemies yanked a thin silver sword off a side hook on the exoskeleton and swung it at James. He caught the blow with his arm, and the sword sank into the armor.

The excited man thought he had gained an advantage. He pulled the blade back and thrust it forward, but this time it bounced off with only a mild gouge. James demonstrated the superior utility of his own blade by slicing the man's arm off and stabbing him through the heart.

Shay found her gun and aimed at the head of one of the distracted assassins. With his helmet and armor, she had a small window for a kill. One shot was all it took, and blood exploded from the side of his head. She'd finished off another man before they realized she was still in the fight.

James cut down man after man, and soon only one assassin remained. He screamed in defiance as he emptied his rifle into his opponent, the bullets accomplishing nothing.

*Huh,* Shay thought. *I wonder if these guys were mercs Fortis hired rather than Fortis agents. It looks like they thought they could win with enough anti-magic defenses.*

James pointed his blade at the other man, who slowly backed up. The assassin pulled out a pistol and started firing. James charged his energy beam and seared the man's head off.

"Damn," Shay muttered. "That'll do it." She reloaded her

gun with conventional rounds before jogging onto the blood-soaked beach.

James kicked at one of the bodies, then stabbed it a few times before turning to maul another, still growling.

*I thought he was more in control than that.*

Shay's stomach twisted. She'd seen him go berserk before, but it never got any easier. Although she never felt unsafe around him when he was like that, she didn't like the idea that he'd lost control, and that maybe Whispy Doom would finally take his chance and take command of their partnership.

"It's over!" Shay shouted. "We're alive, and they're dead."

James swiveled his head her way and stared at her for a moment before his helmet retracted. He took a deep breath. "You're okay?"

"Yeah. I'm okay. One sec; let me try something. Peyton, can you hear me?"

"You're weak, but I can hear you," the hacker responded.

Shay let out a sigh of relief. "I was worried that those assholes were still jamming all the frequencies. I didn't like the idea of having to swim back to the mainland."

The armor began retracting on James as he surveyed the bodies. "I'll give Daniel and his friends credit. They must be running enough interference to keep some of the heat off us. I don't think these guys are Fortis."

"I agree," Shay replied. "But this shit isn't over until we get the map to the Professor."

"If some fucker tries to hijack my plane," James growled, "I will throw him out of it."

"I don't doubt that for a second." Shay grabbed her

satellite phone and winced. Part of the casing was melted and there were scorch marks all over it, but when she pressed a button, it came on. "Good, it's still working. That's easier than having Peyton call. Let me call our ride, then it's just a matter of us here chilling on this lovely beach with the fresh corpses of all the men we just killed."

## CHAPTER NINETEEN

James enjoyed the feel of his F-350's steering wheel under his hands. The last couple of days had involved too much time on planes and boats. A man belonged on land in a good truck, or maybe on a horse.

*Huh. Trucks have horsepower. Maybe that bouncer was onto something. I can't really see me riding a horse, but I could put armor on it. Maybe use magic, carving through fuckers with my blade, all medieval and shit.*

James chuckled.

Shay looked at him with a raised eyebrow. "Care to share the joke?"

"Just stupid shit." James shrugged. "I'll be glad when we drop this map artifact off. Every time I help you out with this kind of thing, I remember how annoying traveling around the world is."

"Sorry we can't drive everywhere. I can't always find jobs near LA." Shay grinned. Her phone rang, and she fished it out of her pocket and lifted it to her ear. "Who is this? Winters? Wait. I'm with James. I'm going to put you on speaker." She lowered the phone and switched it to speakerphone. "What do you mean, you fucked up? Explain it to both of us."

James frowned and glanced at the phone.

*Fucked up? Now what? I want this shit over.*

"It's like I was telling you when we helped you out the other night," Daniel explained. "The other guys have a lot of plays going on right now. It turns out some of them were feints. We wasted some resources in some operations, and they were using that so they could gather forces."

"So what?" Shay replied. "We got what we need, and we're about to deliver it. Then this shit will all be over on our end."

Daniel muttered something under his breath. "That's just it. Because we were on their asses, they couldn't get the personnel they needed to shadow you during your trip to Africa."

Shay frowned. "That explains the guys on the island, but otherwise this sounds like a good thing. If they don't have the personnel to shadow us and we got what we were looking for, what's the problem? I'm sorry they played you a little, but we did what we needed to on our end."

James grunted.

*Other shit always happens when you're involved with the government. What's next? Do we have to go to Mars?*

Daniel sighed. "The truth is, they were reserving the last of their major field forces to throw at you. They'll do whatever it takes to stop you and get the map. They are on their way toward you at this very moment, and they will kill anyone who gets in their way, civilian or otherwise. We can run interference on our end if you don't want the local cops to show up, or we can shove them toward you, even if Fortis is trying to block their arrival. We don't have any tactical assets nearby to help you."

"No fucking way," James rumbled. "I don't want some cop getting turned into candy by an alien ray gun. You keep the cops away, and we'll handle the rest. This shit is annoying, but we've already beat Fortis, and it's time we gave them their final fucking lesson."

"Good luck, Shay," Daniel replied. "Good luck, Brownstone. It might not be much consolation, but if you take these guys out, Fortis is all but finished."

James scoffed. "'If?' There's no chance they'll win against us."

"I forgot who I was talking to. Okay, I'll let you go, and I'll have my people reroute traffic and keep the cops away."

The call ended.

Shay groaned. "We should have stopped off at Warehouse Five to pick up my *tachi*. It's like the universe is conspiring against me lately."

"We're too far away now. If Fortis is already on their way, they might attack the Leanan Sidhe directly if we turn." James gritted his teeth. "Fuck. I'm going to shove whatever alien sword or gun or fancy magical flintlock they're using this time so far up their asses it'll be sticking out of their throats before they die. These guys are really, really annoying."

"You better let the Professor know," Shay pointed out.

James grabbed his phone and dialed the Professor on speaker.

"Good evening, lad!" Smite-Williams answered. "I look

forward to you and Miz Carson's imminent delivery. You can have a pint on me. Consider it a bonus."

"Do you have some way to make this line secure?" James asked.

The Professor sighed. "Aye, I do. The fact that you're asking lets me know what you're about to say. One moment." A few seconds passed. "We're safe now from even the most prying ears."

"Fortis is coming for the map in a big way," James explained. "I'm not sure how you want to play this. We can head toward the Leanan Sidhe, give you the artifact, and try to drive them off from there, or Shay and I can go somewhere else and fight them there. We've got people already rerouting traffic and keeping the cops away just in case, but we don't know if Fortis will follow us if we break off."

The Professor chuckled. "My, my, how very fancy of you. I do appreciate the concern about collateral damage. If you're keeping the police away and rerouting traffic, that makes it simple. I simply need to get all the innocent people out of this area, and we can fight them here."

"We?" Shay echoed. "You're gonna fight, old man?"

"It doesn't seem like I have much choice now, do I, Miz Carson? These very unpleasant men are causing trouble on this job."

Shay sighed. "No offense, Professor. I'm sure you kicked a lot of ass back in the day, but these Fortis guys aren't exactly cannon-fodder. You get involved in this, you might end up dead."

The Professor clucked his tongue. "Sometimes, Miz Carson, age and experience trump the vigor of youth. I assure you that I'll take a few of these men with me if they attempt to take me out, and if I die today, it'll be the most glorious death ever."

"Your funeral," Shay grumped.

"Just hurry to the pub. How prepared are you for the ambush in terms of equipment and general loadout?"

Shay sighed. "I'm down a few weapons I would have liked, but we've got James, so we're bringing a nuke to a knife fight."

"Aye, that's true. Don't worry, Miz Carson. I've got a few things I can lend you. See you soon." The Professor ended the call.

Shay looked at James. "Should we call Heather and Peyton?"

James shook his head. "Daniel's handling the kind of shit they might be able to help with, and by the time they got a drone over here, it'd probably be too late. That's assuming Fortis doesn't jam the whole fucking place again. Let them sit this one out. We'll just party with the Professor. Tonight, though, we end this shit."

CHAPTER TWENTY

When they pulled up in front of the Leanan Sidhe, there were almost no other cars on the street and not a single person around.

"I don't think I've ever seen it so dead," James muttered, unsettled.

Shay tilted her head. "Hear that?"

James listened for a moment. There was faint music. He killed the engine and opened the door. The music was a slow, haunting fiddle melody. When he stepped out of the car, he spotted the source, a fiddle hovering in front of the Leanan Sidhe and playing itself.

"What the fuck is that?" he muttered. "I better not have to do any challenging the Devil shit. I don't mind kicking his ass, but this is California, not Georgia. We don't fiddle against the Devil here."

"I don't think you're going to have to play the fiddle against the Devil anytime soon, as entertaining as that image is." Shay hopped out of the truck. "I assume it's some sort of artifact the Professor is using to repel people."

"Shit's getting weird." James shook his head.

Shay laughed. "Weirder than us getting caught up in fighting a rogue CIA group that is dead set on stopping us from delivering a map to a magical flying castle?"

James grunted. "Maybe." He'd already bonded Whispy. The symbiont hummed with anticipation of the coming battle but otherwise was strangely silent. James stepped toward the front door of the pub and opened it.

Again, he was unsettled. The place was completely empty except for the Professor, who was sitting at a large table in the center.

A light golden nimbus surrounded him. He was wearing multiple rings and some sort of necklace of chicken bones, and he was polishing a tall golden trident. A short sword made of blue-gray mottled metal sat on the table, along with several empty mugs.

"Good evening, lad," the Professor offered, his red face filled with cheer. "It's been a long time since I was involved in a good scrape. This will be as invigorating as a good dirty limerick, assuming I don't die."

Shay snorted. "And if you die?"

"If I die, I've had a good run, Miz Carson, and I'll die knowing I left the world a better place than when I came into it." The Professor gave a cheerful shrug. "Can a man ask for more?"

*I wonder if that shit's the same for me.*

James nodded to the front door. "The fiddle making people stay away?"

"Aye."

"Why didn't it stop us?" Shay asked. "Can it stop Fortis?"

The Professor set the butt of the trident on the floor. "No, unfortunately. It can't stop them for the same reason you're here. It doesn't work on people overly focused on a particular violent goal." He sighed. "I've always known this day would come, but don't worry. Even if you wreck something or they do, I've got more than enough zeroes in my account to rebuild the old girl. I'm not going to let my place die tonight."

James and Shay exchanged looks.

"Wait, you own this place?" James asked.

The Professor beamed a bright smile at him, as if he were preparing for his birthday and not a deadly fight against ruthless rogue CIA agents. "Aye. Did I never mention that?"

"I kind of suspected," Shay commented. "And I'm assuming you have some sort of secure vault around."

"Oh, and then some, Miz Carson, but before you ask, it's not as if I'm keeping dangerous artifacts here at the pub for more than a day after delivery. I just keep a few toys on hand for this kind of situation."

The Professor gestured to the sword. "Sword or trident, Miz Carson? The trident shoots lightning. The sword shoots arrows of light. Both are great at piercing defenses, and they stab well enough as well."

Shay walked over to the table and picked up the sword. It was surprisingly light. "I'm better with swords. I can't even remember if I've ever handled a trident."

"Excellent. The activation phrase is 'lux.' And I see you have your engagement gifts."

Shay nodded. "Yeah. This should be good. Could use a

bulletproof vest if they have anti-magics, but this will stop the worst of it."

The Professor grabbed a mug and headed behind the bar to the tap. He filled his mug. "Do either of you want a drink before all of this?"

James shook his head. "I'm good."

*That man would drink in the middle of a nuclear war.*

Shay shrugged. "Me too."

The Professor finished filling his mug and took a long swig. "I'm assuming, lad, that you'll be using your own equipment? I can grab a few other things if you need them."

James nodded. "Yeah. I'm good. No, wait. You got any shit you don't mind if it gets broken? It doesn't have to be a weapon, just anything with a decent amount of magic."

"Aye. What do you intend to do?" The Professor's eyes turned curious.

"Compensate for not being pissed," James explained.

"Well, now. That's rather cryptic."

Shay activated her defensive artifacts. James was the only one in the room who wasn't glowing.

A bell in the corner of the pub jingled.

James blinked. "Huh. I didn't even think that bell worked. I thought it was just for decoration."

The Professor finished his drink and set his mug down. He walked over to pick up the trident. "It's an overly complicated proximity alarm. I've not had much use for it since it draws attention to itself, but it does mean our friends are close."

Shay reached into her pocket and pulled out the map sphere. "Where should I put this?"

The Professor set the trident back on the table and took the glass sphere out of her hand. "I'll go put this somewhere to keep it secure. I'll note that 'secure' in this sense means it'll only slow down a dedicated group like Fortis. If we die out there, they'll get to it, I imagine."

"Cheery."

The Professor grinned. "Simple solution: we don't die. I'll grab a few things I don't mind losing per James' mysterious request while I'm back there." He hurried toward a hallway in the back and disappeared down it.

James shook his head. "Harriken, cartel, assassins, aliens, fucking rogue CIA alien hunter. How the fuck did my life get so complicated? I used to just be a man with a dog."

Shay laughed as she took a few test swings with the sword. "You're an alien with an adapting super-symbiont. You were kind of doomed, James. Superman has to deal with shit because of who he is. Same thing with you."

"I'm not Superman."

"You prefer Moses?" Shay grinned.

James frowned at her.

"Strength calls to strength, whether to challenge or defend." Shay inspected the blade closely. "Shit, it even brought us together. Would you have liked it if your life stayed simple but you had never met me? Never met Alison?"

The bell rang again, this time louder.

James shook his head. "No, I suppose I wouldn't."

"Then embrace the annoying complexity of life. When assholes show up, we put them down. Eventually, everyone's gonna learn their lesson. Some people are just stupider than others."

"Even the Nine Systems Alliance and the Vax?"

*Achieve maximum adaptation,* Whispy chimed in, an almost wistful undertone to the thought. *Achieve primary directive.*

*You know which directive I've chosen, don't you?*

*Destroy all Vax symbionts,* Whispy responded.

*That's fucking right. I'm not gonna go looking for trouble, but if they show up, they die. You got a problem with that?*

*Maximum adaptation potential would come from battling other Vax.*

*You don't give a shit as long as you're the King of the Hill? Fine by me. You're not Coach anymore, Whispy. You're my partner.*

*Engage and kill enemies,* Whispy responded. *Achieve maximum adaptation. Become the strongest.*

James grunted, a slight smile coming to his face.

Shay's grin turned hungry, knocking James out of his mental conversation. "James, you kick so much ass that I'm hoping in a few years, there's not a single asshole in the entire galaxy who thinks fucking with you is a good idea."

"Yeah, I think Whispy agrees with you."

The Professor emerged from the hallway and laughed. "That would be convenient for both you and the Earth." He held two cracked wooden sticks in his hand. "These aren't weapons, but they do have a decent amount of magical healing power. He handed them to James.

"And you don't care if I destroy them?" James eyed the other man, his eyebrows raised in question. "I need them kind of as fuel."

"Desperate circumstances, lad." The Professor reached into his pocket and pulled out a pair of torn black leather gloves. They glowed for a moment when he slipped them on.

James slipped the sticks under his shirt and placed them against his amulet.

*Let's do it.*

His armor covered him, and his blade extended.

The bell rang a third time, this time so hard it almost vibrated free of its wall hook.

The Professor stared at him, faint surprise on his face. "Knowing about something and seeing it up close are two separate things. It's unfortunate that these lads coming to attack us couldn't see it our way." He nodded toward the door. "Should we go greet our adoring fans?"

"Yeah," James rumbled. He stomped to the door and threw it open. Shay and the Professor followed.

Several vans pulled to a stop on either side of the street, men piling out with various weapons. James saw several more blast pistols and one of the super-rifles he'd faced on the hill.

"I'll go left," he rumbled. "I'm immune to everything they've got, and I've got to take out that weird molecular change rifle before he hits you."

Shay pointed her sword in the opposite direction. The Professor aimed the trident as well.

"Three," James counted. "Two, one…" He yelled in challenge and charged the Fortis agents.

"Lux!" Shay shouted. Three massive arrows of light appeared and flew toward the men. Their van proved useless as cover when the arrows shot through the metal and slammed into one man. An anti-magic deflector around his neck darkened, and he stumbled back.

The Professor spouted something that sounded like ancient Greek to Shay. A massive bolt of lightning blasted from the trident and struck one of the vans, knocking it into the air in a shower of sparks. The anti-magic deflectors didn't help the men crushed by the falling vehicle.

James continued toward the other men. Beams of different colors blasted at him—blue, red, green—none doing much to harm him.

*Near maximum adaptation achieved,* Whispy reported.

Another man aimed a crossbow and fired. The bolt slammed into James and exploded, flinging him into the air along with a shower of asphalt but not doing much to hurt him. He landed a few seconds later and rolled back to his feet with a growl.

The man with the molecular transformation rifle aimed the weapon at James and pulled the trigger. The air wavered around James, but nothing happened. The man blinked in disbelief.

James continued to close on the agents, who were now less than ten yards away.

The agents on the other side desperately tried to return fire, but the near-constant barrages from Shay and the Professor weren't giving them much opportunity. One man squeezed off a blast pistol shot at the Professor, the blue beam striking the man, but his golden aura dimmed for only a second and his smile grew wider before he returned fire with a lightning bolt that charred his attacker.

"Aye, I had forgotten how much fun this could be," the old man shouted.

James reached the agents, ignoring everyone except the man with the rifle.

The agent backpedaled and tripped, pulling the trigger. One of the agents nearby screamed for a second before he turned into a twisted mass of tangled limbs.

The agent scrambled to his feet and fired the rifle again, this time not at James, but the van behind him. Tentacles sprouted from the side of the vehicle, and a huge gaping maw filled with metal teeth opened on its side. A row of eyes appeared near the roof.

*What? Is it like whatever the fuckers are thinking of?*

James ignored the new monster to stab the man through the chest before taking the rifle and crushing a nearby man's head with it. A black tentacle snatched the weapon from his hand and tossed it into the mouth. Several more tentacles snagged the avenging bounty hunter and tugged him toward the maw.

The Fortis agents continued to fire their energy weapons at the restrained James. The man with the crossbow loaded in a new bolt and fired it into his chest. The explosion knocked him right into the mouth of the van-turned-monster.

The creature clamped down around him, a thick, viscous liquid filling the small space James occupied. The liquid hissed on contact with the rifle, burning it and the few remnants of cloth left on James.

*What? Acid? That shit is weak.*

James thrust his blade into the roof of the mouth and carved an exit. Fleshy black tissue fell in, the entire creature thrashing as he climbed out the top and jumped into the surviving agents.

The heavy beat of approaching rotors came from the south.

*Fucking Daniel. You were supposed to keep the cops away from here. Now we've got to end this shit before they get hurt.*

The combined assaults of Shay and the Professor had finished off almost everyone on the opposite side. A last barrage killed the two remaining agents.

"I'm liking this sword, Professor," Shay commented. "Maybe I should buy it from you."

He replied with a merry laugh. "Shake a leg, Miz Carson. We're not done yet, and I'll have you know that weapon takes decades to charge. You've used up centuries of its power already."

"Shit. Sorry."

James eviscerated his final enemy with a grunt.

*Low adaptation potential,* Whispy complained.

James turned and jogged around the bodies toward Shay and the Professor. Both were breathing hard and covered in sweat, and the glowing auras that marked their defensive artifacts had dimmed, but neither seemed hurt.

"You finished over here?" he rumbled.

Shay waved her sword. "Yeah, looks like it. Sounds like the cops are coming."

Multiple helicopters flew closer, along with a duller roar.

"Oh, shit," James muttered as he looked up. They weren't police helicopters.

*Engage and kill stronger enemies for maximum adaptation,* Whispy offered, excitement rising again in the symbiont.

Two black helicopters appeared overhead. One held a half-dozen men wearing silver gauntlets on one hand. The side doors were open.

In the other helicopter, a suited man raised a small silver disc and pressed a button on top. He threw it toward the front of the Leanan Sidhe.

James, Shay and the Professor all jumped to the side as a white-blue explosion went off a few yards above them.

CHAPTER TWENTY-ONE

The attack knocked James down and through the front of the Leanan Sidhe. He rolled, hissing, actual pain registering in his mind.

*Shit. Guess Fortis* did *have a few surprises left.*

*Yesssss,* Whispy sent. *Adaptation in progress. Regeneration in progress.*

James blinked his eyes. His armor was cracked and charred, and mild burns covered his exposed face. He shook his head and stood.

The Professor lay face-down, burns all over his body and much of his clothing incinerated. His arm was bent at an unnatural angle.

*No, no, no. No fucking way.*

James let out a roar of anger. A pile of rubble moved and Shay popped up, her skin back to its normal color and cuts covering her face. There were rips all over her clothes.

Shay rushed over to the Professor and turned him face-up. His skin was battered and burnt, but he was still breathing.

"He's still alive. I'll take care of him." Shay reached into her pocket to pull out a healing potion. "You keep them off us." She threw herself over his body as another explosion blasted apart the remaining front walls of the Leanan Sidhe. One of the ceiling fans crashed to the ground.

Shay pulled the wounded Professor around the corner of the bar as James stomped forward, his body trembling with anger.

*Sufficient energy for extended advanced transformation.*

This anger tasted different. Cold, but just as powerful.

*Do it,* James sent.

He continued striding forward, most of his armor restored between his regeneration and transformation. Two of the silver-gauntleted men stood across the street, and a third was making his way down a nylon line from the hovering helicopter. The other helicopter remained closer to the Leanan Sidhe, or what remained of it.

A third explosive was thrown from the helicopter, and James leapt into the air toward the device, grabbing it and continuing upward. The aircraft rose in the sky as the explosive went off, this time barely scorching him and knocking him back to the ground. He smashed into the sidewalk, leaving a huge crack in the pavement.

The silver-gauntleted agents finished unloading. James ignored them and raised his arm. He took a few seconds to charge up as the vehicle attempted to escape. His attack separated the rotor from the rest of the craft, and the helicopter tumbled to the street and exploded in a shower of glass and metal.

The other helicopter quickly gained altitude. James growled and jumped into the air as he charged his beam. At the height of his arc, he was far from the fleeing helicopter, but it didn't matter. The shot tunneled through the center of the craft and blew it to pieces.

James landed on the ground only a few yards away from a gauntlet agent, flaming helicopter debris raining down around them.

*Moderate adaptation potential,* Whispy suggested.

One of the men lifted his gauntleted hand. The light curved and wavered around it. He grinned. "We underestimated how quickly you can adapt, Brownstone, but that's not going to happen this time."

James growled. Despite the anger flowing through him, his focus remained on the enemy. They would pay for what they had done to the Professor. He'd make sure of it.

Another man lifted his hand, shadows covering it.

The others lifted their hands, in turn producing flame, haze, an opaque pulsating orange miasma, and crackling electricity.

None of the men advanced. "Killing you—an alien infiltrator who hid here for decades while he gathered the strength to undermine our planet—will be Fortis' ultimate achievement."

"Fuck you," James rumbled. "You guys couldn't win even with your magic monster guns. You're a bunch of fucking idiots."

"Magic monster guns? Ah, a weapon that you have to concentrate on too much to use isn't a good weapon. It's not reliable. A *good* weapon can be used even by a scared soldier."

"You're not a soldier," replied James, his voice low and full of murderous promise. "You're nothing but a bunch of killers telling yourselves that because you work for the government, everything you do is all right. I've saved more people in my life than all of you pieces of shit combined, and you're all gonna die here."

*Kill the enemy*, Whispy chanted.

*I want to kill their spirits first.*

The cold anger continued to flow through him, simmering at the edge of control. He was tired of self-righteous assholes fucking with him and the people around him. Fortis didn't have to be his enemy. If they wanted to take on the Vax and the Nine Systems Alliance, they could have even been his ally, but now they had threatened his friends and blown up the Leanan Sidhe. They had to pay.

The men all charged James at once. He didn't bother to dodge. They all threw a fist, each covered with a different type of attack energy at him. The blows struck in unison, and he jerked once, a slight jolt passing through him.

*Near maximum adaptation already achieved. Kill the enemy. Find stronger enemies.*

They jumped back, surprise on their faces.

James turned toward the man who had spoken earlier. "Don't know where you stole that shit, but I've been exposed to a lot of things, and my adaptation isn't temporary. What, you assholes thought as long as you used a bunch of different attacks, it'd work?" He let out a low growl. "It's your worst nightmare, Fortis. I don't know if there's anyone left on Earth who can take me down when I'm pissed off." He sprang forward and slashed in a wide arc, his blade slashing deep into the throats of two men and the chest of a third.

The three other men charged him, the various energy

fields pulsating around their gauntlets. They threw punches at James, but their blows bounced off. He barely noticed. He cut down two more men before grabbing the last man by the throat and lifting him.

"Figure it out, assholes. The only option left now is to point the monster at the other monster." He dropped the man to his knees and tore his throat out with his claws.

The Fortis agent fell backward, gasping and clawing at his wounded throat, his blood draining out and coating the street.

*Kill the enemy*, Whispy sent *Become the strongest.*

James threw back his head and let out a long, loud snarl.

*Wait*, James thought. *Shay. The Professor.*

He turned and rushed toward the smoking wreckage of the front of the Leanan Sidhe. Some of the anger started to flow away. His helmet and blade retracted as he stepped back inside.

The Professor sat at a table with a beer in front of him and a smile on his face. His clothes and hair were still torn up, but his wounds were healed. "Share a beer with me now, lad?"

James stared at the man. "The Leanan Sidhe is totaled, there's a bunch of dead guys in the street, and you nearly died, and you think it's time for a beer?"

"You don't understand, lad." The Professor gestured around the bar. "I'll rebuild this place. I've got more than enough money to do that, and it gives me a few months to visit some people I've been meaning to go see. Losing half a bar in the process of making sure the appropriate artifacts get to the appropriate people is a small price to pay, and as for beer? Well, it's *always* time for a beer."

Shay leaned against the smoldering bar, her arms folded over her chest. "There's going to be a lot of explaining to do."

"I'll mostly leave that to the man who hired me, but I've accumulated more than a few connections throughout the last couple of decades who can help." The Professor picked up the beer and took a sip. "Danger and death always await us. Why worry about the expected? The important thing is that you got that map, and I'll be able to collect the vimana, and most of the men who think nothing of murdering innocent people are now dead."

James' armor retracted, leaving him nearly naked.

The Professor chuckled. "Never thought I'd need to have extra trousers on standby. I'll keep that in mind for the future, lad."

# CHAPTER TWENTY-TWO

When the knock came at James' door the next day, he considered bonding Whispy. Even though the Professor and Shay seemed convinced everything was over, he wasn't sure. He walked to the front door and activated the front door camera. A handsome dark-haired man in his thirties was standing there in a suit.

His posture was too perfect, and his eyes were too suspicious. The man was obviously a government agent. James' hand curled into a fist. He would twist any Fortis agent into a pretzel if they damaged his house.

His phone chimed with a message from Shay.

**Visitor should be at your front door. I've vetted him.**

James put his phone back in his pocket and opened the front door. "Who are you?"

"Daniel Winters," the man explained with a too-practiced smile. The voice matched what James had heard in the truck.

James pointed to his couch. "Take a seat."

Daniel stepped inside. "Do you mind if I use an anti-snooping device?" he asked after James closed the door.

James shrugged. "I don't give much of a shit either way."

The CIA agent removed a small silver cube and set it on James' coffee table before taking a seat. "I figured we should meet."

"Why?" James asked as he walked over to his recliner and sat down.

Thomas had returned to his spot beside the chair after the flurry of barking at the front door.

"I'd like to be on good terms with you, Mr. Brownstone," Daniel explained. "I'm assuming you understand the big picture of what occurred by now."

James grunted. "Far as I can tell, someone in the government hired the Professor to have Shay go get the vimana map so the Professor and some other people can go grab the vimana. The idea is they can have some big flying castle to fight spaceships or shit, but these Fortis assholes, they wanted control of it, so they tried to kill Shay and me."

"That's a pretty accurate and to-the-point understanding of the overall situation," Daniel replied. "Specifically, it was Senator Johnston, who I'm sure by now you appreciate is a pretty significant player in the United States' response to alien threats."

James narrowed his eyes. "I've got one question. Did he know about Fortis?"

Daniel sighed. "He was initially supportive of them, actually, until they went too far."

"You mean killed random people to cover their shit up," James muttered.

Daniel's face darkened. "Exactly. He then became key in helping support other factions who wanted a more balanced approach, such as the one I'm associated with."

James shook his head. "All this shit is too complicated. He could have come to me directly."

"Sometimes a few layers of plausible deniability mean survival in government, especially government black ops. I just thought you deserved to know. It's not an exaggeration to say you're at the center of all these events even if you're not the only alien concern."

"You talking about the Nine Systems Alliance?"

Daniel chuckled. "Of all the threats I've dealt with in my recent career, they're actually on the more reasonable side. At least we know where they're coming from. No. The Vax and the Alliance aren't the only groups of aliens out there, or even the only groups who have messed around with aliens. You dealt with it. You saw some of the salvaged tech taken from other alien races. It's advanced even compared to the Alliance."

"You mean those weird-ass rifles?"

"Exactly." Daniel took a deep breath. "Some things are too dangerous. I used to think those things represented some of the most dangerous alien tech on Earth. You saw what they can do: transmute matter based on thought alone."

James narrowed his eyes. "Used to think?"

"My people have collected some of the footage taken from cameras near your last fight with Fortis." Disbelief spread over Daniel's face. "You were able to take shots from them like they were nothing. You should be dead or a pile of peanut butter, or something."

"The first time I got shot with one it turned my arm into stinking purple smoke." James grunted. "That shit wasn't fun."

"But you have two arms…" Daniel blinked and looked at each of James' arms. "I see. That's even more impressive. I understand now why you're such a vital part of Senator Johnston's alien defense plans."

"What about you, CIA?" James rumbled. "You just basically said I'm scarier than your magic monster gun. Does that mean you're gonna come at me soon, just like all these other fuckers?"

"No. You see, I've dealt with a lot of aliens directly, and it's taught me an important lesson."

"What's that? Don't start shit you can't finish?"

"My grandfather taught me that long before I joined the CIA." A genuine smile appeared on Daniel's face. "The lesson I learned is that aliens are a lot like anyone from Earth or Oriceran. Some are good. Some are bad. Most are complicated."

James snorted. "And you're saying I'm good?"

"I'm saying you're a man with deep ties to this planet and no ties to wherever the hell the Vax are from. You're also a man who could easily have followed the path of a criminal or a mercenary selling his talents and abilities to the highest bidder, but you didn't. You're a man who still faithfully attends his church and gives money to orphans."

"You know all that? CIA's really up my ass, aren't they?"

Daniel chuckled. "Most of that we got from the NSA, but the point is, Mr. Brownstone, it's never what a man says that's important. It's what he does."

James snorted. "You expect me to be impressed? If you

guys had minded your own house, we wouldn't have had to deal with Fortis. It's gonna take months to repair the Leanan Sidhe, and the Professor almost got killed."

Daniel's smile disappeared, replaced by a stern frown. "And I'm sorry for that. You're right. You've done us a great service by helping us all but finish off Fortis. I'll be honest. If they had gotten their hands on the vimana, given how ruthless they are, who knows what they might have done with it? The kind of men who'll kill innocent people to cover up a secret are not the kind of men I'd trust with access to an artifact like that."

"Yeah, not saying I disagree." James put up his footrest. No reason he couldn't relax why he was being debriefed by this CIA agent over his involvement in fighting another CIA faction. "But now that everyone knows the fucking truth, maybe you can answer a question for me? And don't feed me any 'it's classified' shit."

"I'll do my best to answer. That's all I can promise." Daniel shrugged.

"You guys aren't going around killing people like Fortis, but you're still keeping shit secret."

"You're not exactly announcing to the world that you're an alien," Daniel replied.

James scoffed. "Because I don't want fuckers like Fortis coming after me and blowing up my favorite restaurants and bars. What's the government's excuse? Oriceran is weirder than the idea of aliens from space. Why the big cover-up? People can handle it. The last couple of decades proves it."

Daniel let out a low chuckle. "People could handle it, sure. People could handle the concept of aliens from space.

That wouldn't change anything. And you're right, Oriceran is weirder, but there have been a decent number of magicals on Earth forever, and we have organizations like the PDA to offset them, let alone bounty hunters like you." He leaned forward, all the humor gone. The man could turn it on and off in an instant. "Now imagine people find out that the aliens could park a ship in orbit and wipe Los Angeles off the map, and even with magic, we might not be able to do much about it. It'd make the chaos after the gates reopening look like nothing. I'm sure the truth will come out within the next few decades, but for now, we've got to ease into it, until we can honestly tell people, not just in America, but across the entire world, 'Don't worry. We can protect you.'"

*We can protect you.*

James could understand the sentiment. He might not be the smartest man or the most educated, but he was strong, and he'd always thought he could protect everything and everyone important to him. The Harriken made him realize he'd been wrong, but since then, he'd done everything he could to ensure that kind of loss would never happen again.

James grunted. "The fight we had with Fortis was pretty messy. Tons of dead bodies. Crashed helicopters, an entire building half-destroyed. How are you covering all that up? When I fought the Council, the government just admitted what happened."

"It's not like anyone, regardless of faction, wants to admit that rogue CIA operatives basically started a major battle in the middle of Los Angeles. If it wasn't for Professor Smite-Williams' quick thinking with that fiddle artifact, hundreds of people could have ended up hurt. There are many layers of government using their influence to make certain evidence go away, such as traffic camera and drone footage, but you need to also be on board, because your name is in the middle of the cover-up."

James slammed the footrest down. "What the fuck?"

Thomas popped his head up for a moment, looked at James, and then snuggled back down to sleep, completely ignoring the stranger in the room.

"You're fundamentally an honest man, Mr. Brownstone," Daniel explained. "That means you don't know how to lie well. You're probably decent at lying through omission, but I'm a spy. I'm great at lying. I was trained to be great at it, so let me give you a little helpful hint. The best lies, the ones people are willing to swallow without pushing too deep, are those with a core of truth."

"What's the core of truth this time?" James rumbled.

"That you fought some men near the Leanan Sidhe, and you killed those men." Daniel shrugged. "Just a few details have been changed. It wasn't Fortis agents you fought according to everyone including the LAPD, it was overzealous cartel members who thought they could kill James Brownstone, but because of your concern about casualties, you made sure that one of your contacts cleared out the area." He shook his finger. "Let me make this clear: this is the official story, and the chief of police is playing ball even though he doesn't know the full story. The media is already being supplied with evidence that corroborates that version of events, so when they contact you, just grunt and tell them you killed the guys trying to kill you."

James scoffed. "I knew getting involved in government

shit would be annoying."

"Hey, imagine how I feel! This is my day job." Daniel offered him a playful smile, but James wasn't in the mood.

"Is this shit over then? I thought it was after the first attacks, but they came at us twice after that."

"My people have been able to account for the vast majority of missing agents who allegedly died in the plane crash I told Shay about. I'm not going to blow smoke up your ass and tell you that Fortis has been eliminated, but they no longer have any effective field operatives." Daniel stood and dusted his hands on his pants. "And that means my people can handle them from here and keep them from bothering people not in the game—like you."

James locked eyes with Daniel. "So Fortis is done, but what about the rest of you? You said you trust me, but what if you get the call to take down James Brownstone next week? You gonna be a good little soldier and come after me?"

Daniel headed toward the door without a response, but stopped and looked back at James when he reached it. "For now, I believe you're a man who will defend the United States, so I'm not going to worry about that."

"And if that ever changes?"

"Let's just say I've got a few more tricks and favors I can call in that even Fortis and Senator Johnston don't know about." Daniel opened the door. "With any luck, neither of us will ever see each other again. Have a good day, Mr. Brownstone." He stepped outside and closed the door.

James grunted.

*I can't figure out if I like that guy's attitude or if I want to punch him in the face.*

## CHAPTER TWENTY-THREE

The Professor sighed as he settled into the booth of the pub with a fresh mug of beer. It was a nice enough place, but it wasn't *his* place.

*We all suffer in the long fight. At least I'm still breathing.*

An unassuming Light Elf in a hoodie walked up to his booth and took a seat.

The Professor eyed the elf and smiled. "New look, Correk?"

"It involves a bet with Leira." Correk frowned. "Don't ask."

The Professor reached into his coat pocket and pulled out the small glass sphere that had cost so many lives. He handed it to the elf. "This would all have been far easier if you had been directly involved."

"I'm the Fixer. My purview is the protection of magicals, not getting involved in internal US intelligence struggles." Correk frowned.

"Oh, don't feed me that, old friend." The Professor pointed at the sphere. "We both know what that represents. The fate of Earth and all the magicals on it is tied to how well we're able to defend it. If this planet ceases to exist, it's going to be rather nasty for the magicals on it, and the Oricerans who will need to come to it."

"It's all paranoia, though. You have no proof that anything's going to happen. If the Nine Systems Alliance wanted to go after Brownstone, they've had months to do it."

The Professor shook his head. "I wish I could share that optimism, but all I can do is assume that the aliens are as moral as humans."

Correk winced. "That bad?"

"Aye." The Professor lifted the mug to his lips and took a sip. The beer outside of the Leanan Sidhe didn't taste as satisfying. "But I understand your restrictions as Fixer. All I'd like to know is if you think we'll actually be able to activate the vimana."

Correk took a deep breath and looked down for a long moment before giving a slight nod of his head. "Yes. Everything you've collected and you've had Shay get for you should be enough. I just hope we'll never have to use it."

"You and me both, old friend. You and me both."

---

James leaned back in the confessional booth, pressing his back against the cool wood. "Bless me, Father, for I have sinned. It's been two weeks since my last confession."

"What do you have to share with me today?" Father McCartney replied.

"I've kept a grave secret from you, one that might affect

my soul. I've thought long and hard about it, but some recent events make me think I should tell you the truth."

The priest sighed. "James, honesty is important in the sacrament. I'm surprised to hear that you have been keeping secrets, given all the other things you've told me."

James' hands curled into fists. "This isn't something I've always known, and it might be dangerous for you to know. I'm gonna say this now. If there's any government ass… government agents listening to this, and anything happens to this man after I tell him, you'll see the full power of a Vax."

"Vax?" Father McCartney echoed. "Government agents? I don't know what's going on, James, but I don't want you to endanger your soul because you think you're protecting me. I'm willing to take the risk."

"I'm not human, Father," James replied. "I didn't know before, but now I know."

Father McCartney sighed. "That's your secret?"

"You don't sound surprised." James blinked.

"You do things that no normal man can. There's no shame in being from Oriceran. I've long suspected it."

James shook his head. "No, you don't understand. I'm not from Oriceran. I'm an alien from a race called the Vax, and they aren't the only ones out there. The government's keeping them a secret because they're not sure if there will be a panic."

Father McCartney took a few moments to digest the news. "Somehow none of that surprises me, nor does it change anything."

James chuckled. "It doesn't change anything that I'm not human?"

"The Lord created all of the universe, not just Earth," the priest replied softly. "I know everyone's still arguing about the metaphysics of it all, but that's my belief. As such, I don't see that it's relevant what species you are, as long as you are faithful. Also, this sacrament is sacred, so none of what you've told me here will be spread beyond this confessional."

"Huh."

"What troubles you now?" Father McCartney asked with a faint hint of amusement in his voice.

"I just didn't think this conversation would go like this. I didn't even tell Shay about it." James leaned forward. "Just between sh…stuff that's happened in the last couple of weeks and the wedding coming up in the summer, I want to be right with you and the church."

"As I've told you before, James, you're a good man. I still believe you're a good man, no matter what planet you were born on."

Shay eyed James from her side of the bed. "You did *what?*"

"I told Father McCartney the truth. It's not a big deal. He took it well."

Shay scrubbed a hand over her face. "That could have backfired in a big way."

"Maybe." James slipped the amulet off his neck and set it on the nightstand next to him. "But the less I have to lie, the better. The government knowing all that shit made a lot of what had to go down easier. It's not like I'm planning to go on some news show and have them broadcast that

I'm a Vax Forerunner, but if I can tell people I trust, why not?"

Shay sighed. "I suppose. Maybe someday you will be able to tell everyone. Are you going to tell Alison?"

"Yeah. She needs to know, and anyway, she might already have figured it out. Saw it in my soul or some shit. I'll give her a call soon. I just want to make sure all this vimana and Fortis shit isn't as fresh. I don't want her asking the right questions and figuring out what went down. Somehow she always seems to be able to tell if I'm holding back, even over the phone."

Shay snickered. "The truth is, James, you're just a terrible liar."

James chuckled. "CIA Boy said something like that."

"It's not a bad thing. You're a straightforward guy, and even if you hide the amulet, it's not like you're much for bullshit misdirection. It's one of the reasons you drove me nuts when I first met you. Every man like you I've met before *has* been into bullshit misdirection, so when you dealt with me honestly and openly, it confused the hell out of me. I kept trying to understand your angle."

James grunted. "Yeah, and kept assuming I was gay."

Shay gave him a sheepish smile. "You're not the only one who needed to learn how to deal with people better, you know." She leaned back and rested her head on her pillow. "I wonder if the Professor and a bunch of wizards are out in the desert somewhere raising a vimana. I always assumed he already had it, but now that I know he didn't, it's... Shit. It's a little cool. I still doubt they'll be able to do much with something that was made during an age of high magic, but if they dump enough magic into it, maybe they can accomplish at least a little with it. But that's the kind of thing that—I don't know—really makes you think about how things were back on Earth then. It's almost as if they were more impressive than on Oriceran."

"What? You saying all this getting shot at by Fortis shit is inspiring?"

Shay laughed. "Yeah, I guess it is."

"And what is it inspiring you to do?"

"Epic wedding venues."

James shot up, his heart pounding. "Meaning what?"

"I'm just saying that a wedding on the ground would be kind of boring. Everyone does that shit."

James stared at her, uncomprehending.

"I'm not saying that I want a vimana wedding," Shay clarified. "But maybe something in the air. There has to be some way to manage it. We've both got plenty of money and magical contacts."

James shook his head. "If God wanted man to fl—"

"He would have given them wings. Blah, blah." Shay rolled her eyes. "I wonder what stupid shit arpaks say that sound like that. What about a plane?"

"You know I hate them, too."

Shay's breath caught. "Underwater wedding. I bet that's easier. I'm sure you get a few elves and wizards together, they cast a spell and make a little air bubble or some shit."

James grunted, unsure if Shay was being serious or teasing him.

*Underwater wedding? I guess it's better than a gnome bounce castle on the moon.*

CHAPTER TWENTY-FOUR

Sentry 8224 tapped his AllBand a few times to verify that the long-range comm link was stable before clearing his throat.

"Reporting, Sentry 8224, Senior Shepherd Corayailaxi Jakimalitta, in response to the last inquiry sent by Command. I am confident that my time on Earth has given me sufficient information to place the actions of Sentry 7921 in proper context, while also providing recommendations for future Alliance interactions with Earth." He waited until a telltale beep indicated the words had been processed. "Let me first note that I agree with earlier conclusions that Shepherd 7921's actions were excessive, and on multiple occasions, she clearly harmed innocent natives outside the scope of her operational mission. With that duly noted, the Vax threat represented by James Brownstone is even more extreme than was perceived by the junior Shepherd. In a recent series of encounters with rogue intelligence agents of the US government, the Vax, operating in armored mode, was able to survive attacks by a molecular rearrangement weapon associated with an unknown advanced species. I'll be looking into them further to determine their influence and threat to Earth."

He tapped his AllBand a few more times to send along some images he had intercepted of James battling Fortis agents outside the Leanan Sidhe.

"In addition, there is little evidence that any tactical-scale magic or technology available on Earth presents a serious threat to Brownstone any longer, including most of the tactical-scale weapons available to the Alliance. Therefore, it is imperative that the humans agree that we take possession of Brownstone. Without the support of his government and with surprise, it might be possible to capture Brownstone. Since the humans obviously don't trust the Alliance, it is my recommendation that we provide them with a technology sample that proves our good intentions. Altering the course of their technological development wouldn't violate general policies, given that the course of their history has already been heavily manipulated by the open use of magic."

Sentry 8224 took a deep breath, unsure of his next statement, but also understanding it was where the evidence led him.

"Lastly, it is my recommendation that a fleet presence be established in this system until such time as we take custody of James Brownstone or he's killed. After analyzing human technology and magic in addition to reviewing Sentry 7921's reports, I believe that it should be easy to conceal a number of ships as long as we keep them in the outer system. Their technological detection methods remain crude, and their experiments suggest that the range and power of magical spells is limited off Earth. Please note; it is important that we conceal the fleet. The humans will not knowingly tolerate the presence of a fleet in their system."

A few firm confirmatory beeps issued from the AllBand and he transmitted the message. It was up to his superiors now.

---

The Vax knelt in front of the central spire of the Temple, his eyes closed as he murmured a prayer. As First, it was his solemn duty to lead and protect his people the best way he knew how: by cleansing the galaxy of all threats.

The last few cycles had gone well. Only a few Forerunners had failed. Most had sent out their pulses, and the Vanguard had gone to meet them. Death had followed. The cleansing of worlds that might threaten his people continued. The Culling Path continued to protect them.

Light footsteps sounded behind the First.

He opened his eyes but didn't turn around. "What is it?"

"I apologize for disrupting your prayers, First, but an unusual signal was detected."

"A Forerunner calls for the Vanguard?" The First stood and turned to stare at the robed Vax behind him.

"No. The signature was Forerunner energy, but it wasn't a hyperspace pulse."

The First narrowed his eyes. Many of the technical details of the Culling Path eluded him, as did those of the bonded. When he was younger, it had bothered him, but now he had faith that every Vax had a part to play. His was to lead, not to understand the minutiae of hyperspace pulses.

"Clarify," he demanded. "And be efficient about it, servitor."

The other Vax blinked his yellow eyes a few times. "It's…you see… We believe a Forerunner used transformation abilities near existing portals, perhaps those generated by other races. Somehow it resonated in a way that we were able to detect it, as if the signal was amplified."

"Other races with portal technology?" The First shook his head. "This isn't acceptable. They must be Culled. They are a threat to our people and our planet. Why hasn't the Forerunner called for the Vanguard if he's using his abilities?"

"That's the other important finding," the servitor explained. "Given what we detected, we believe this is the Heretic Child."

The First's breath caught. He almost fell to his knees to weep at the good fortune bestowed on them. The years might have passed, but the Heretic Child had never left his thoughts. His parents might have paid with their lives, but they'd wasted a Forerunner and sent him off to some unknown place.

"It will be difficult, First, but from what I've been told, we can use this resonance to track the Heretic Child," the servitor continued. "But we need your permission to send the Vanguard."

"No." The First shook his head. "The purity of the Heretic Child is questionable."

"But he's using transformation abilities. He is a bonded, then, and performing his duty as part of the Culling Path."

The First turned back toward the spire. "We cannot be sure his symbiont rules him. Send a Purifier. Once he has found the Heretic Child, he will call the Destroyers directly to Cull the world."

The servitor gasped but didn't say anything. The First knew what he was thinking. His plan varied from the official Culling Path dogma, but some perversions couldn't be allowed to exist.

"Conflict comes from impurity," the First intoned. "Purity breeds strength. And strength will protect the Vax."

**THANK YOU for not only reading this story but these *Author Notes* as well.**

(I think I've been good with always opening with "thank you." If not, I need to edit the other *Author Notes*!)

**RANDOM (*sometimes*) THOUGHTS?**

I know I mentioned in the last *Author Notes* (I think) that we are doing a Brownstone-type series with another character in his <redacted> in the <redacted>. That person is a <redacted> and will handle the situations as they pop up, similar to Officer <redacted> during the event at <redacted>.

I hope you look forward to it!

Another James Brownstone idea we are tossing around is a road trip series. Maybe a book every 3-4 months when James goes on the road for BBQ and busting someone's ass.

I like to think of it as a kick-ass road trip series.

You know, James gets bored, decides to try some

Kansas City BBQ, and then someone does something stupid around him while he is there?

Let us know what you think of that idea on the Facebook Group for Oriceran:

https://www.facebook.com/OriceranUniverse/

In a couple of days, my wife and I are going to have dinner with Mark Dawson and his wife at their home in Salisbury, England. Mark offered to meet us someplace else since their town is where the Russian agents killed someone with horrific poison that sticks around. I explained I wasn't too concerned if those who lived in the city were dealing with it just fine.

Something new, something old.

For those who have read enough of my author notes, you know I am a Texan by birth and lived there most of my life.

You don't just drop the attitude.

## AROUND THE WORLD IN 80 DAYS

One of the interesting (at least to me) aspects of my life is the ability to work from anywhere and at any time. In the future, I hope to re-read my own *Author Notes* and remember my life as a diary entry.

### London, England

I'm looking out the window at Big Ben (most of it is covered up as they work on it, but the clock face is almost staring right at me.) We are here for the London Book Fair, which is starting next week.

I can't honestly tell you what else I have to do today since my mind is goop. The trip from Las Vegas to New York and then New York to London went well enough, but I'm wondering if the height the planes fly is causing me breathing issues.

I just find it harder to breath up in the air.

## FAN PRICING

$0.99 Saturdays (new LMBPN stuff) and $0.99 Wednesday (both LMBPN books and friends of LMBPN books.) Get great stuff from us and others at tantalizing prices.

Go ahead. I bet you can't read just one.

Sign up here: http://lmbpn.com/email/.

## HOW TO MARKET FOR BOOKS YOU LOVE

Review them so others have your thoughts, and tell friends and the dogs of your enemies (because who wants to talk to enemies?)... *Enough said ;-)*

Ad Aeternitatem,

Michael Anderle

OTHER SERIES IN THE ORICERAN
UNIVERSE:


**Other series in the Oriceran Universe:**
THE DANIEL CODEX SERIES
I FEAR NO EVIL
THE UNBELIEVABLE MR. BROWNSTONE
SCHOOL OF NECESSARY MAGIC
THE LEIRA CHRONICLES
REWRITING JUSTICE
THE KACY CHRONICLES
MIDWEST MAGIC CHRONICLES
SOUL STONE MAGE
THE FAIRHAVEN CHRONICLES

OTHER BOOKS BY JUDITH BERENS

BOOKS BY MICHAEL ANDERLE

For a complete list of books by Michael Anderle, please visit

**www.lmbpn.com/ma-books/**

All LMBPN Audiobooks are Available at Audible.com and iTunes. For a complete list of audiobooks visit:

**www.lmbpn.com/audible**

CONNECT WITH MICHAEL ANDERLE

**Michael Anderle Social**
**Website:**
http://www.lmbpn.com

**Email List:**
http://lmbpn.com/email/

**Facebook Here:**
https://www.facebook.com/OriceranUniverse/
https://www.
facebook.com/TheKurtherianGambitBooks/

www.ingramcontent.com/pod-product-compliance
Lightning Source LLC
Chambersburg PA
CBHW050239110726
47898CB00007B/2210